SMUGGLER

SMUGGLER

RICHARD CARPENTER

Illustrated by Graham Humphries

An Armada Original

Smuggler was first published in the U.K. in 1981
in Armada by Fontana Paperbacks, 14 St. James's Place,
London SW1A 1PS.

Printed in Great Britain by
Love & Malcomson Ltd., Brighton Road,
Redhill, Surrey.

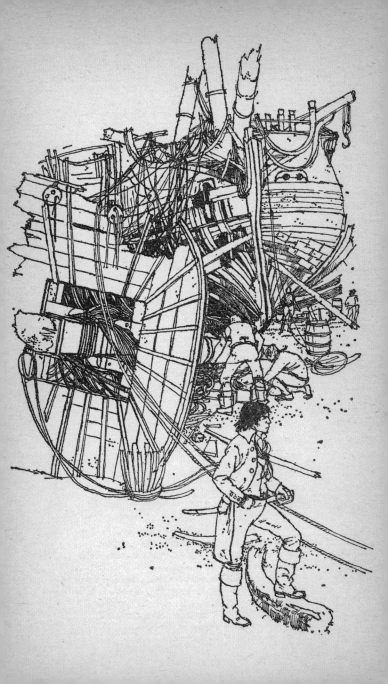

CHAPTER ONE

IT was a night of storms along the southern coasts of England. The seas raged and seemed to boil against the cliffs, and scores of ships ran before the gale, seeking shelter in every harbour. Lookouts peered anxiously from the crowsnests into the rain-filled darkness, watching for the faint light from beacons, warning them away from the rocks.

The *City of Bristol* – a merchantman crowded with immigrants bound for Canada – rolled in the huge waves off Quayhaven. Her captain was the first to see the distant beacon flickering from the cliffs and he silently thanked the good people of Quayhaven for their help. He was taking his ship away from the warning light when suddenly she seemed to shudder throughout her length, and with a rending and splintering of timbers, crashed on to the fang-like rocks.

The sea swept in and instantly every light was extinguished. Men, women and children screamed in terror as they were hurled against bulk-heads and crushed in the roaring dark. Some fought their way up to the tilting deck and leapt into mountainous waves. The *City of Bristol* keeled over and began to break up. As her captain was sucked down into the icy blackness his last thought was that the beacon had been meant to deceive him. It had been placed there by those most evil of men – the wreckers!

The storm blew itself out before dawn. Along the rocky foreshore, little knots of people moved like feeding gulls among the splintered planks and riven timbers of the wreck. Boxes and barrels littered the bay and bobbed in towards the eager scavengers. On the beach, Silas Kemble strode among the villagers of Quayhaven, barking his orders and watching carefully as the carts were loaded and hurriedly driven away. Nothing escaped his sharp eyes.

Outwardly, Silas seemed a bluff and jovial man, but his heart was as cold and as merciless as the sea. As well as landlord of The Raven Inn on the Exeter road, apparently a good-natured host, he was also the leader of the Gallants, a band of fishermen and farm workers secretly engaged in the dangerous business of smuggling.

The early years of the nineteenth century had seen a vast increase in illegal trade. The war with Revolutionary France had ground to a halt with the Treaty of Amiens in 1801: but wars had to be paid for and so the British Government had raised the taxes, or 'duties', on goods coming from abroad – most importantly on tobacco, brandy and tea.

To avoid paying these 'duties', cargoes were landed in secret and sold to the public without the knowledge of the officers of the Customs Service. These men were the smugglers' enemies and often fought pitched battles with them. They had power to search ships at sea, or 'rummage' them, and they could also investigate any cargo after it reached port.

The smugglers waged an endless war against the Customs men and succeeded in landing boatload after boatload of 'duty-free' goods. They ran them ashore at dead of night on lonely and inaccessible beaches, and stored them anywhere they could: in haystacks and pig-sties; in churches and stables. Anywhere in fact, away from the eyes of the Revenue men.

Silas had been a smuggler all his life. At one time, he and his men had been regarded as benefactors by the rest of the community, but the years had made them greedy.

Now the money he made from smuggling wasn't enough to satisfy him and he had turned to the murderous business of wrecking. Silas controlled most of the smuggling in the borough and the ordinary people feared him. At night, wearing masks, and smocks to hide their clothes, he and his Gallants would go about their secret trade and heaven help anyone who tried to hinder them!

His brother William stood beside him on the beach. He was younger than Silas; a thin, ill-looking fellow, liable to fly into sudden and uncontrollable rages. William took great pleasure in torturing anyone who refused to help the Gallants. Many people whispered that he was insane.

Silas looked out to sea.

"No survivors . . . God rest their souls."

"A good night's work, eh, brother?" muttered William with a wolfish grin.

Silas turned to him and smiled. "A dangerous bit of coast – this is," he said.

"Someone must've moved the beacon," replied William.

Silas looked up towards the top of the cliff where the fire was still burning in an iron brazier.

"Now who'd do a thing like that?" he said with an evil grin.

The last of the carts trundled away across the beach and William turned to a ragged man who was searching through the pockets of a sodden coat.

"That's mine," he snarled.

"It ain't, you lying swab," replied the man, edging away.

"You can have the buttons," said William softly, moving nearer.

"Buttons, my eye!" the man spat at him, "I want the blessed coat!"

William grabbed hold of the coat and for a moment the two of them struggled for possession, their boots slipping on the wet rocks.

"A sail!" shouted the man, suddenly looking out to sea.

"You won't catch me like that!" snarled William.

"Look, man!"

Still holding on to the coat, William Kemble swung round and looked out across the bay.

Round the point came a small, single-masted lugger with a tall figure at the tiller.

"That ain't the Revenue cutter!" sneered William. "That's Jack Vincent."

But nevertheless, the two men stopped struggling for the coat and ran for the shelter of the rocks.

Aboard the lugger – the *Mary Jane* – Jack Vincent looked bitterly at the wreckage floating in the waters of the bay. He was a dark, saturnine, handsome man with tangled black hair and several days' growth of beard. He wore the rough clothes of a fisherman and his long sea boots were streaked white where the salt water had dried on them. In his wide belt he carried a cutlass.

Jack was enraged by what he saw. He knew that scores of innocent people had died that night to put money into the Kemble's pockets.

William and his ragged companion watched as the little boat came into the shore.

"Back from Guernsey, I'll wager!" William whispered.

The lugger reached shallow water and Jack lowered the sail. Then he jumped out and pushed the boat in through the waves until it grounded. He slung a small anchor into the beach and then walked over to the cart-tracks and examined them. Then he looked round him: the Kembles had made a thorough job of it: the wreckage on the fore-shore had been picked clean. Had there been any survivors? He doubted it. Those that had survived the waves had probably had their throats cut as they stumbled, exhausted, through the breakers.

On some half-submerged rocks, some way down the bay,

there was a tangle of spars and cordage. Part of a sail was flapping in the stiff breeze; but something else was moving among the wreckage and Jack began to run.

When he was opposite the rocky outcrop, he waded into the water and hauled himself on to the slippery rocks. Clambering along them he reached the pile of wreckage and looked down at it. An arm stuck out from underneath part of a sail: it was moving feebly. Jack pulled the sodden sail and ropes to one side and revealed the body of a young lad.

The boy was pathetically thin and a lank mop of fair hair hung over his pale forehead. Jack judged him to be about fourteen. His ragged clothes clung to his meagre form, but though he was bruised and bleeding and half-drowned, he was still alive. His leg was trapped under a spar and Jack strained to lift it away. Then he picked him up and carried him slowly to the beach. He laid him gently down in the shelter of his boat and crouched beside him. The boy stirred. As he did so a shadow fell across him and Jack swung round.

He was not a moment too soon. William Kemble's cutlass sliced through the air, missing him by a hair's breadth, and sank deep into the lugger's gunwhale.

Jack was on his feet in a moment as the other villain ran to help William. Drawing his cutlass, he parried left and right as the two men cut at him in quick succession, but his swordsmanship was more than a match for both of them. A savage cut opened William's shoulder to the bone, and with a howl he dropped his sword and clutched the wound. His companion, realising that he faced Jack alone, backed off immediately.

William sobbed with pain.

"We ain't finished with you, Jack Vincent!" he cried.

For answer, Jack advanced on them again, and the two men took to their heels. At a safe distance, William turned

11

again and his envenomed voice rose to a scream which sent the sea birds wheeling high above the cliffs.

"Your time's a-comin', Vincent. Make no mistake o'that! It's run out for you, matey, you'll see! You'll see!"

Jack said nothing, but he continued to watch them until they disappeared round the distant headland. Then he picked up the boy and carried him in among the rocks under the cliff and entered a small cave.

The Quayhaven cliffs were honeycombed with a bewildering maze of passages and caverns. They ran inland for several miles and had been used by the local people for centuries. But very few knew their full extent as well as Jack Vincent. When he had first come to the borough, three years before, he had spent several months exploring with a compass. He had mapped each cavern and passageway, until he knew every twist and turn of that rocky warren. During his explorations he came across an iron ladder leading up a rocky shaft, placed there by smugglers of an earlier time. At the top of the shaft, Jack had found a chamber beneath the chimney stack of a ruined cottage perched high on the cliff-top. Its stone walls had resisted the storms of two hundred years, but the roof had collapsed and lay in a pile of rotting timber and shattered slate. For months, Jack had laboured to repair the cottage, rebuilding the roof from ships' timbers he found in the many wrecks along the coast.

Now, in pitch darkness, he carried the boy through the twisting passageways to the iron ladder. Slowly, he climbed the shaft to the secret chamber behind the fireplace. Sliding back a panel, he took the boy into the cottage and laid him gently on the heavy oak table, clearing a place among the bottles and the dirty wooden plates.

He fetched brandy in a cracked cup and put it to the boy's lips, cradling his head in his arm. Most of the spirit trickled down his chin, but eventually the lad began to

12

cough and his eyes flickered open and took in his surroundings.

The interior of the cottage consisted of a single room. At one end, steps led up to a kind of platform where Jack had his bed. The single door was of oak and very solid, and led directly out into the yard. On either side of it were two small windows, and a lantern hung from a hook from one of the ceiling beams. By the fire was a large leather armchair, torn and sagging. Nets, ropes and a sail were stacked untidily against the walls. The only other piece of furniture was an old dresser, littered with bowls and saucepans and more empty bottles. The flagged floor was unswept and cobwebs hung everywhere.

The boy looked up at Jack and muttered in Welsh.

"D'you speak English, boy?" said Jack quietly.

The boy nodded. "English. Aye. The ship . . ."

"It broke up on the rocks."

Again the boy muttered in Welsh.

"English, boy," Jack repeated.

"I remember," muttered the boy, coughing up more water. "It was terrible – the sea was terrible!" He began to shiver uncontrollably. "By God, I'm as cold as death!"

Jack brought blankets and rekindled the dying fire. He sat the boy in front of it and listened to his story.

"We was going to Canada, see?" whispered the boy, warming his bruised hands. "Start a new life, me dad said. The whole family was going. Me dad . . . me mam . . . Powis . . . Rose . . . and the baby . . ." He stared into the flames.

"What's your name?" asked Jack, breaking the silence.

"Honesty," said the boy. "Honesty Evans." His blue eyes stared into the fire. "Are they – ?" He broke off and then, after a moment, tried again. "Am I alone now?" he said in little more than a whisper.

Jack got to his feet and put his hand on the boy's

shoulder. He could say nothing to comfort him; he knew that there was little likelihood his family had survived.

"Try to sleep," he said.

The boy looked away and his eyelids drooped. The brandy and the warmth from the fire were beginning to make him drowsy: soon he would be asleep. So Jack, who was anxious to secure his cargo – bales of silk from St Malo – climbed back through the secret entrance, quietly shutting it behind him.

For some minutes, the boy dozed fitfully in front of the fire, but his natural curiosity got the better of his tiredness, and he got to his feet and padded round the cottage, poking and prying into every corner. The ladder to Jack's bed intrigued him most and, after glancing carefully around to make sure he was alone, he climbed up it for a closer look.

A small window overlooked the sea. On the wall beside it hung an aquatint of a ship in a storm. There was a small chest of drawers, with a model of a man-of-war standing on it. There was also a cracked mirror.

The boy pulled open the drawers one by one but found nothing except some old clothes and sheets. Disappointed, he turned and began to examine the bed. There was a chest underneath it, and he pulled it out to have a closer look. Painted on the lid were the words *Lieutenant J. Vincent, H.M.S. CASSANDRA*. The chest was padlocked.

The boy grinned and took a curious-looking tool from the pocket of his ragged trousers. It was a pick-lock. He worked busily for a while, then the padlock sprang open and he threw back the lid.

A naval sword lay on top of an officer's uniform. Honesty lifted the sword and began drawing it from its scabbard.

"*Put it back!*" roared Jack Vincent, who had returned through the secret entrance and silently climbed the ladder.

The boy dropped the sword as if it was red-hot, and jumped up. Jack Vincent faced him, trembling with rage.

"I was – I was only – " began the boy.

"Downstairs!" ordered Jack in tones that brooked no denial.

The boy shot down the ladder and darted round the far side of the table for safety. Jack slammed the chest shut, shoved it back under the bed with his foot, and followed him down the ladder.

"How did you open it?" he asked quietly.

The boy looked at him with innocent blue eyes.

"Oh, it wasn't locked," he said.

"*It's always locked*!"

Jack looked dangerous. The boy evidently decided that perhaps it was safer to tell the truth.

"I picked it," he confessed. "With this." And he held up the pick-lock. Jack took it from him.

"And your name is Honesty Evans!" he remarked bitterly.

"Are you – Lieutenant Vincent?" asked Honesty, hastily changing the subject.

"I'm a fisherman," he said flatly.

They were interrupted by a knock at the door, and with a warning glance to Honesty, Jack opened it. Mr Cooper, the local tailor, and a garrulous little man, peered up at him. He had come to buy some silk.

"Not late, I hope, Mr Vincent?" he said, rubbing his hands nervously and glancing across at Honesty, who was still wrapped in the blanket.

"He's from last night's wreck," explained Jack.

"Terrible," groaned Mr Cooper sympathetically. "Very few survivors, I believe. Very few!"

Jack picked up two small bales and carried them outside to the tailor's cart. Mr Cooper bustled after him, carefully closing the door. Jack undid one of the bales to reveal a bolt of silk.

"Fine quality, Mr Vincent," murmured Cooper, fingering the material with professional skill. "Ten guineas?"

"Twelve."

"Then twelve it shall be," Cooper agreed, and counted a dozen coins into Jack's palm.

"A very fair price," he said. "Life's hard enough for a tailor without such a terrible tax on silk. You're an honourable man, sir, and I'm grateful to you."

"If you're as silent as you're grateful," said Jack with a smile, "there could be more."

"I can be silent as the grave," replied Cooper blandly. "As the grave, Mr Vincent."

He helped Jack cover the bales under a tarpaulin, and climbed on to the driving platform of his little trap.

"What'll you do with the boy?" he asked curiously.

"There's a workhouse in Quayhaven," replied Jack. "That's unless you need an apprentice," he added ironically.

"Oh, don't wish him on me, Mr Vincent," said the tailor hastily. "I've two already – both good-for-nothings. The young people today! They've no application, you know – no industry. I would suggest that you take him to Westmore Hall. Old Captain Konig's a kindly man, and I believe they're looking for a stableboy."

"Captain Konig?" queried Jack.

"A German," Cooper went on. "He was a ship-owner in London. He bought the Hall some years back. His wife was English I believe. Now he lives there alone with his grand-daughter. Well, I hope to hear from you in the not-too-distant future – eh, Mr Vincent?"

Jack nodded, and went back inside the cottage as the trap moved off along the cliff path.

Mr Cooper was congratulating himself on his good

business as he drove along the road to Quayhaven when he suddenly found his way barred by a group of Silas Kemble's men and forced to rein his horse.

"Silas wants to see you," said one of them curtly. Cooper trembled. He didn't relish a meeting with the leader of the Gallants, but he knew better than to disobey.

Silas had been aware of Jack's activities for some time. The man was undercutting him and taking away his trade. He hadn't sold Cooper any silk for months, and when he looked in his leather-bound account book he noticed that a local storekeeper – Mr Davidson – had stopped buying tobacco. It seemed that various other merchants and inn-keepers were no longer buying his contraband. So where were they getting it from? Silas was certain that his hold on the borough was being weakened and undermined by the activities of Jack Vincent. He was determined to put a stop to them.

The terrified Cooper was carried into The Raven and dumped unceremoniously on a large barrel standing in front of William and Silas Kemble. In silence, the leader of the Gallants examined the bales of silk, while Cooper waited anxiously.

"Nice bit of stuff," growled Silas. He looked benignly down at Cooper. "Lived here all your life haven't you, Mr Cooper?"

Cooper nodded.

"Then you know the way things are around these parts. You're one of us. We all help each other. Like a family, ain't we?" Silas moved closer to the terrified tailor. "Now this Jack Vincent. Where do he come from, eh? I ask you – who is he? He ain't one of us! He don't belong here, do he? All he does is make trouble for me and my lads. And now he's making trouble for you, Mr Cooper, ain't he? If you want to buy silk, you know where to come. Or lace, or 'baccy, or anything else you want. But it must be

17

at the right price." Silas grinned. "Now that's not unreasonable, is it? Not considering the nature of the trade, and the wheels that have to be greased. You do see that, don't you, Mr Cooper?"

"Yes – yes, Mr Kemble," agreed Cooper nervously.

"Oh, I knew you would," smiled Silas. He turned to a serving wench. "Fetch Mr Cooper a drink, Mary. He looks a bit pale."

Th girl hurried to get the tailor a glass of brandy while Silas opened his account book and put on a pair of spectacles which gave him an almost fatherly expression. One of the Gallants brought him an inkwell and a quill pen.

"Now these bales here," said Silas in a business-like tone, "are going to cost you twenty guineas."

Cooper looked horrified. "But I've already bought them!" he explained.

"Not from me," said Silas firmly.

"They're my property!"

"*Contraband*!" roared Silas.

"But this is – this is – " stuttered Cooper helplessly.

"Business, Mr Cooper," replied Silas easily. "Business."

"But I can't afford it!" gasped the tailor.

"Then you'll have to go without!" snarled Silas. He grabbed the brandy from Cooper's hand and drank it himself. Then the Gallants lifted the wretched man off the barrel, carried him to the door, opened it and hurled him out into the muddy road. Silas, William and the rest of them roared with laughter.

"And now it's time we had a talk with Jack Vincent," muttered Silas savagely.

CHAPTER TWO

WESTMORE HALL stood amid a group of elm trees on the edge of the moor. It was a grey, somewhat forbidding building, with high chimneys. Wide buttresses supported the walls against the coastal gales, giving it a fortress-like appearance. Huddled round the Hall were stables, two shepherd's cottages and an ancient barn. Behind it, the moor stretched away into the distance.

Jack had decided to heed Mr Cooper's advice, and so with Honesty in tow he walked across the moor from his cottage to see if Captain Konig was still looking for a stable-boy. Honesty, however, didn't like the idea at all, and told Jack so with considerable indignation both in English and in Welsh. But despite entreaties and curses in both languages Jack remained adamant. Whatever happened, Honesty was not going to stay with him.

He hammered on the door of Westmore Hall, and after a moment it was opened by a servant who looked at him with disdain.

"I wish to speak to Captain Konig," said Jack.

"Captain Konig cannot be disturbed," replied the servant loftily.

"Oh, can't he?" replied Jack, sticking his foot in the closing door. Still holding Honesty, he pushed past the servant and entered the Hall.

"Come back!" shouted the enraged servant. Jack ignored him and walked purposefully onwards.

"Captain Konig!" he called loudly.

He had reached the foot of the stairs leading down to the hall when a girl appeared on the landing and glared down at him.

19

"Who are you, sir?" she said angrily.

She was beautiful, thought Jack. She had small delicate features but there was nothing insipid about her. Her eyes were dark and seemed to flash fire as she waited impatiently for his answer.

"Tell your master I want to see him," Jack replied.

"My grandfather is asleep," the girl answered indignantly and hurried down the stairs. "And I –"

"Then wake him up," interrupted Jack.

"Naylor – put this man out!" she said angrily.

The servant came forward nervously and hesitated.

"Come on, Naylor," Jack invited with an amused grin. "You heard the young lady."

"Shall I get help, Miss Sarah?" Naylor asked, eyeing Jack apprehensively.

Jack turned back to Sarah. "This boy's from the wreck. His family were drowned."

She looked at Honesty, who immediately put on a suitably pathetic expression. Sarah remembered how her own parents had been drowned in a terrible storm some twelve years ago, and her heart softened towards the boy.

"Oh, the poor lad," she said sadly. Then she looked at Jack. "This way," she commanded coolly.

They followed her to the door of Captain Konig's study, where she told them to wait, and disappeared inside.

"It's like a palace, this place!" breathed Honesty, looking round with amazement. "They must be ever so rich, don't you think?"

"You keep your hands in your pockets," replied Jack shortly.

"Why does he need such a big house to live in, eh?" Honesty continued. "You could keep twenty or thirty cows in here."

The door opened and Sarah beckoned them inside.

Captain Konig's study told Jack a great deal about the

man: a man whose whole life had been the sea, ships and their cargo. It was full of memories, as well as all the practical projects on which the captain was engaged. There were paintings of the four ships he had once owned, and a portrait of himself with his wife and daughter. There was a globe of the world and a large brass telescope on a mahogany stand near the window. Several coastal maps could be seen on the walls, and on the large desk were even more, all neatly rolled and tied. There was a fine sextant, and pens and brushes in a Chinese jar. In a glass case was a collection of shells and pieces of coral. The room also had several flags displayed, and the bookshelves contained numerous books on navigation and the history of seamanship.

The captain, a weather-beaten man in his late sixties wearing an old-fashioned, navy-blue velvet coat, rose as Jack and Honesty entered the room.

"Well now, my good sir," he asked courteously, "how did you save this boy?"

Jack was impressed by Captain Konig. He knew that his own appearance was unprepossessing but he was being treated as an equal. The girl, Sarah, however, obviously disapproved of him – not that he cared.

"I didn't save him," said Jack abruptly. "I found him."

Captain Konig ignored Jack's brusque manner, and turned to Honesty.

"What's your name, boy?" he asked.

"Honesty, sir. Honesty Evans."

"And yours?" asked Konig, looking at the swarthy figure before him.

"Jack Vincent."

Sarah looked at him with horror. So this was the notorious Jack Vincent! His exploits were known throughout the borough. He spent his time in the taverns down in the harbour: he would drink until he was insensible and gamble until his pockets were empty. Silas Kemble's bullies had attacked him several times but had found him too tough for them. He was a dangerous adventurer who defied authority and lived a strange, hermit-like existence in a lonely cliff-top cottage.

But Sarah had also heard of his kindness to local fishermen, fallen on hard times. He'd been known to give them money to repair their boats, battered by the heavy seas; he bought them nets and new sails and tubs of brandy to warm their hearts.

It was common knowledge that Jack Vincent was more than just a fisherman who sold his catches in the Quayhaven market: the stories of his smuggling tricks were endless, and he was known to have outwitted Mr Marwood, the Customs Officer, on many occasions.

Sarah remained staring at Jack while her grandfather nodded imperturbably.

"Vincent, eh?" he replied easily. "I knew a Vincent. A Captain Vincent. He was killed at the battle of Les Saintes, off Dominica in 1782."

Jack thought it better to ignore this reference to his father, and returned to the subject of Honesty. "I heard you were looking for a stable-boy," he said.

Captain Konig poured a glass of brandy and held it out to Jack with a smile. "The position is already filled," he said. "Why not let him work for you?"

Sarah could contain herself no longer.

"Grandfather – this man's a smuggler!" she exclaimed.

"You've a damned long tongue!" said Jack.

"Everyone knows," she went on. "It's the talk of the borough."

Jack held up his glass of brandy to the light. "Did Mr Cooper make that dress?" he murmured. "I wonder where he got the cloth?"

Sarah blushed in confusion, and Jack faced her grandfather again.

"The boy's no use to me," he said. "You deal with him as best you can. You can afford to."

He tossed back the brandy, put down the glass and walked to the door.

"This is outrageous!" fumed Sarah.

"So are high prices and heavy duties," retorted Jack. "But they don't affect you, do they?"

"What do you mean, sir?" asked Captain Konig indignantly.

"You can afford to pay 'em. The mass of people can't. There's whole catches of fish rotting on the quay because fishermen can't buy salt. There's children running half naked because of the price of cloth – "

"I'm aware of the unfairness of the present system," Captain Konig replied.

"Are you?" said Jack evenly. "Good."

Then, without waiting for Konig to reply, he left the room abruptly. Sarah stood stunned by such blunt bad manners, and then ran after him.

Captain Konig shook his head, amused rather than angered. He looked at Honesty who had taken advantage of the argument, and had been surreptitiously filching several little objects from the desk. "Put the paper-weight back, Master Evans," he said. "And the other things if you please."

Honesty, who prided himself on his skill as a sneak-thief, was amazed that the old gentleman had noticed. Meekly, he began to unload his pockets.

Captain Konig smiled. "Perhaps we can make something of you, eh," he said gently.

Meanwhile, Sarah had caught up with Jack in the hall and faced him furiously.

"How dare you speak to my grandfather like that!" she stormed.

"I'll speak to whom I like, how I like!" replied Jack, opening the front door.

"Not in this house, you scoundrel!"

"I'd rather be a scoundrel than a hypocrite," retorted Jack, stepping outside.

"I haven't finished," Sarah went on angrily. "You are an ill-mannered boor with no respect – "

"Respect?" interrupted Jack, his eyes suddenly angry. "I've shown respect, madam. A damn sight too much respect. It's what people are, not what they wear, or the houses they live in – "

"That's enough!"

"Quite enough," said Jack, and marched away from the house, leaving Sarah shaken by his vehemence and wondering why she was so upset by it.

Jack walked home slowly across the moor. The girl's beauty and her passionate nature had affected him strongly. Despite his anger, he wanted to see her again. The wind was rising and dark clouds were gathering over the sea. The weather mirrored his mood and he felt lonelier than ever. For hours he sat on the cliffs watching the waves beating endlessly, with senseless fury, against the rocks below.

Night was falling as he approached his cottage. Suddenly he noticed the door was ajar. Always alert to danger, he crept up to it quietly and threw it open.

Honesty Evans was making soup by the fire.

"I didn't really like that big house, Mr Vincent," he said calmly, stirring the pot. "And that old German! I've never heard such stories! You couldn't believe a word of them."

"I locked this door," said Jack slowly.

"I know you did," replied Honesty.

24

"You picked the lock!"

"No, Mr Vincent," said Honesty, holding up Jack's key. "I picked your pocket!"

Before Jack could grab him the boy dodged round the table.

"Don't be angry, Mister Vincent!" he begged. "I'll tell the truth now, I promise. Only please don't hit me!"

"The truth?" said Jack.

Honesty nodded.

"I never had a family on that ship. Never had a family ever. Only aunties. Not real aunties, mind. There's lots of lads like me around the docks. I stowed away, I did."

"Stowed away?" said Jack incredulously.

"Yes. Thought I'd try my luck in Canada. They were after me, you see."

"Who were?"

Honesty smiled wanly. "Just about everybody!"

There was a pause. The only sound in the little cottage was the moaning of the wind and the soup bubbling in the pot. Honesty looked slyly at Jack. "I'd even thought of joining the navy," he said.

"Oh did you?" smiled Jack grimly.

"You were in the navy, weren't you?"

"The whole damn family was in the navy," muttered Jack. He stared out of the window, remembering how only three years earlier during the war with France he had stood at a Court of Inquiry and received a reprimand for putting his ship at hazard. The reprimand caused him to resign his commission in the navy and cut himself off from his family and friends. He had disobeyed an order, it was true, but he had sunk a French frigate – a bigger ship than the *Cassandra* – and he was damned if he would take a reprimand for that . . .

He was brought back to the present when he saw the Kembles and their men creeping through the bracken towards the cottage. He grabbed hold of Honesty and bundled him across to the secret entrance. He pushed him inside and shut the panel. The next moment the Gallants rushed in and overwhelmed him. Silas gave a nod and his men tied Jack's hands behind his back. Calmly, Silas pulled out a chair from the table and sat himself down.

"You've been running silk, ain't you?" he grinned.

Jack remained silent.

"Well, we know you have," he continued. "And what else, eh, Jack? Tea? Snuff? Tobacco?"

Again there was no reply.

"I don't like it, Jack. None of us do!" Silas went on. "Nothing comes in along this part of the coast that we don't handle. We fix the prices and we make the rules."

It was William's turn to come forward. "You been undercutting us, ain't you?" he said.

"You've had warnings and ignored 'em, haven't you?" Silas added.

The Gallants murmured their agreement. It was time to settle accounts.

"There's only one thing to do, ain't there?" said Silas.

"And I want to do it!" cut in William, drawing a long knife from his belt.

Silas laughed gently. "You mustn't mind my little brother, Jack boy," he said. "Bit – hot-headed at times, you know."

"Get on with it!" snarled William.

Silas wagged an admonishing finger at his brother.

"Got to be a proper job, William. A proper job." He turned to his men. "Don't need to vote on it, do we boys?"

There was a chorus of "No" from the Gallants.

"I'd call that pretty unanimous," chuckled Silas. "Wouldn't you, Jack?"

"Go to hell," said Jack.

This seemed to amuse Silas. "No friend," he replied.

"That's where you're going. And the sea will send you there."

In the secret chamber, Honesty listened with horror.

"Gull Rock," said William.

Silas nodded. "Aye. Gull Rock!" He turned to another of his men. "Jacob. Search this place!"

He heaved himself from the chair and strode across to the door and threw it open. "Bring him!" he barked. The Gallants seized Jack and hustled him out of the cottage.

At low tide, Gull Rock stood like a jagged pillar on the wet sands some way to the east of Quayhaven, but when the waves lashed against the rocky cliffs, the sea swept over it and submerged it completely. Smugglers had used Gull Rock for centuries to dispose of their enemies. The bodies were carried out to sea when the tide turned, and no-one was any the wiser.

Jack was tied hand and foot and hauled up to a narrow ledge. A loop of rope was put round an outcrop above his head and this held him in position on the rock. After drowning him, the sea would continue to rise until the loop floated off, freeing the body. The tide would then carry it down Channel and out into the broad Atlantic.

Silas looked at his watch and then up at his victim.

"Tide's just about turning, I reckon," he said calmly. "There's plenty of time for you to make peace with your Maker."

"Amen!" mocked William, with a horrible laugh.

"No hard feelings, lad," smiled Silas. "Would you like a pipe of 'baccy to calm you?"

Jack stared at him, unable to believe that anyone could be so callous. Then he shook his head.

"As you will," said Silas. "May the Lord have mercy on your wretched soul."

The men took off their hats and for a moment stood with their heads bowed as if in prayer. Then, without so much as a backward glance, the entire gang marched off across the sands in the direction of Quayhaven.

Jack watched them go and calmly surveyed his position. If he moved his body, the rope round his neck would strangle him; if his feet slipped off the ledge, the same fate awaited him. He looked down at the rocks some fifteen feet below: already the tide was creeping towards them across the sands.

Back at the cottage, Honesty listened as Jacob, cursing and swearing, ransacked the place. The boy was too terrified to move in case a sound should betray his whereabouts. Presently, he heard the Gallants returning.

"Jack Vincent's getting his feet wet!" It was William's voice.

"In a couple of hours it'll be his head!" laughed Silas. "And when the tide turns tonight, he'll be carried right out to sea – just like all the others. What've you found, Jacob?"

Jacob held up Jack's naval sword.

"Looks like he was in the navy," he said.

"An officer, eh?" muttered Silas. "I might have known it. Found anything else?"

"Nothing," Jacob replied.

"What d'ye mean, nothing?" growled Silas. "This place has been here for a hundred years. Built by smuggling men, I reckon. I've heard tell there's a tunnel to the sea."

This last remark was not lost on Honesty.

"That's a yarn, Silas," sneered Jacob. "An old wives' tale."

"I ain't so sure," Silas persisted. "He must keep his stuff somewhere. And I want to find it and put it alongside ours. At the church."

In the pitch black of the secret chamber, Honesty began to explore. Moving cautiously, he found the top of the iron ladder and climbed down.

When he reached the base of the shaft he groped his way along the tunnel, stopping every few yards to listen for the sound of the sea. Luck, and an instinct for the right direction, led him onwards, and at last distant roaring and a faint light rewarded him.

He emerged among the rocks and stood, dazzled by the bright sunlight, looking cautiously around him. He had to get help, and as quickly as possible, or Jack Vincent would surely drown. He set off along the beach.

An old fisherman was sitting propped up against a rowing boat in a little inlet of the bay, mending his nets. He looked up as Honesty raced towards him.

"You're in a muck sweat, ain't you?" said the old man.

"They've tied Mister Jack to Gull Rock!" gasped Honesty.

"What are you yammering about, boy?"

"We've got to save him," said Honesty. "We've got to! A whole gang of them did it. Broke into his cottage, they did. Their leader's a man called Silas."

The old man nodded.

"Hurry, mister, or he'll drown!"

The old man pulled a pistol from his belt and pointed it at him. "There's no hurry, lad," he chuckled.

Honesty's escape had been in vain. The old fisherman was one of Silas's men, and he took the boy to his leader, who was still trying to find the entrance to the secret chamber.

"Who's this, Benjamin?" he asked, eyeing Honesty suspiciously.

Benjamin grinned. "Comes running up to me yelling that you're a'drowning Jack Vincent."

"Did he now?" breathed Silas, pulling Honesty to within inches of his face. "Now what put that notion in your noddle?"

"Been left out at Gull Rock, he says," said Benjamin.

"Gull Rock? Where's that?" asked Silas with mock innocence.

"Never heard of it," said William.

Honesty pulled himself free and ran to the door, but the Gallants were too quick for him. Then Jacob stepped forward and pointed a finger at him.

"I've seen this sprat before. He's the kid Jack Vincent saved from the sea."

"How do you know about Gull Rock, you little scab?" snarled William.

"Because he's a prying Welsh rabbit, ain't you, boy?"

"Why don't I take him for a walk along the cliffs?" asked William evilly.

"I'll see you all hang," Honesty shouted.

"Oh, will you now?" chuckled Silas. "You'd better take him for that walk, William!"

There was a shout of laughter from the Gallants, and William hauled Honesty out of the cottage.

"Let me go – you English pig! Let me go I say!" shouted Honesty, kicking at William's shins and wriggling like an eel. But the man merely bared his teeth in a savage grin and gripped him even harder.

"I'll let you go all right," he tittered. "Right over the cliff!"

Honesty screamed for help at the top of his voice, but there was no-one to hear him but the gulls. Slowly, William half dragged, half carried him to the edge of the cliff.

"Come on, kid," he whispered. "Not much further!"

Honesty could see the jagged rocks below and the sea crashing against them. Remorselessly, he was forced nearer and nearer to the edge of the cliff. He thrashed about, kicking at William's legs, but they were protected by his heavy sea boots. Then, as the man was forced to change his grip, Honesty seized his chance and sank his

31

teeth into William's hand. With a howl of pain, William let go, and the boy was off like a hare. William fumbled for his pistol, but by the time he had got it from his belt and cocked it, Honesty was out of range. The bullet went wide and, still cursing, William charged after him. But Honesty had been chased before, many times. Most of his life had been spent in the alleys and along the quays of the Bristol docks. There he had learnt to outstrip the most determined of his pursuers.

On he ran, and soon William was left far behind. Honesty slackened his speed and began to look around. He was on the edge of the moor, and ahead he could see the tall grey chimneys of Westmore Hall. He ran faster. Captain Konig would know where Gull Rock was. There was still time to rescue Jack.

Sarah and her grandfather were walking together in the gardens when Honesty ran up to them.

"You've got to help me, Captain Konig!" he panted. "You've got to. It's Mister Jack. They've put him on Gull Rock. A gang of them done it. And when the tide's in – he'll drown!"

"Gull Rock!" gasped Sarah.

"The tide there rises forty feet!" cried Captain Konig.

"Then there's no time to lose!" exclaimed Sarah. "Follow me, Honesty!"

Sarah ran to the stables with the boy at her heels and saddled and bridled her horse as quickly as she could. Then, with Honesty mounted behind her, hanging on grimly, she galloped away from the Hall. The cliff path was narrow and uneven, but she rode at a reckless pace. She could see Gull Rock far out in the bay. Already the sea surrounded it.

By this time the waves had reached Jack's chest. He still fought savagely to free himself. If he could release his hands he knew he still had a chance. But the Kembles had known what they were doing and his frantic struggles made the cords round his wrists even tighter.

Sarah took the path leading down through the rocks and reached the sandy foreshore. Here, Honesty slid to the ground, grateful to be in one piece. He kicked off his shoes and ran into the breakers and began to swim. The tide was running strongly and the waves buffeted him, making his progress painfully slow. Sarah watched anxiously, willing him onwards.

As he drew near Gull Rock, he could see Jack still struggling to free himself. The waves were beginning to break over his head and it would only be a matter of minutes before he was drowned. Honesty redoubled his efforts, thrashing his way through the water.

Jack watched as Honesty swam towards him. He strained to keep his head above water.

"Hallo, Mister Jack!" Honesty shouted cheerfully as he reached him.

"Get on with it!" gasped Jack.

"You'll let me stay with you – won't you?" Honesty pleaded.

"I think I'd rather drown," groaned Jack.

"Then drown, you ungrateful devil!" retorted Honesty and turned away.

"*Cut me loose!*" roared Jack.

" 'Please'," said Honesty.

Jack controlled himself with an effort. "Please," he said.

Honesty grinned and dived like a seal as Jack twisted on the rock to help him. Under water, the boy sawed at the ropes until he was forced to come up for air. Then down he went again. The strong current forced him away from the rock but he worked grimly until his lungs were bursting. But at last the ropes parted and Jack was free.

Together they swam towards the shore.

Sarah ran into the water to help the exhausted pair to safety.

"She brought me here, Mister Jack," said Honesty. "Without Miss Sarah, I'd have been too late!"

Jack stared at Sarah. "Thank you," he said.

"The Kembles may still be at the cottage, Mister Jack," warned Honesty.

"Then you'd better come home with me," said Sarah.

At Westmore Hall, Jack and Honesty sat wrapped in blankets in front of a roaring fire and sipped Captain Konig's finest brandy.

"In the morning," said Sarah, "we will see that the militia arrest the Kembles."

"For what offence, my dear?" replied her grandfather.

Sarah looked at him in some surprise. "Why – for attempted murder."

"No," said Jack.

"I beg your pardon?" said Sarah indignantly.

"The Kembles rule this coast," Jack explained. "And half the borough help them – or suffer the consequences."

"What do you mean?"

"Farmers who refuse to lend them horses find their cattle slaughtered in the fields and their hayricks set on fire. No local jury would convict them. Do you think I'm the first to be put on Gull Rock?"

"So much for free trade!" retorted Sarah bitterly.

Jack smiled. "Besides, it's my word against theirs."

"But I saw you on Gull Rock."

"You never saw the Kembles put me there."

"But I heard everything, Mister Jack," piped up Honesty. "Everything they said. About finding your stuff and putting it with theirs at the church."

Jack looked at him. "What church?" he asked.

Honesty shrugged. "I don't know," he muttered.

"So they use a church, do they?" said Jack slowly.

34

"But what church?" repeated Captain Konig.

"It must be Hallerton," said Jack.

"Why?" asked Sarah.

"Because the belfry was restored a month ago," he explained. "A full peal of eight. And those bells were paid for by the Kembles." He stood up excitedly. "We have them!"

Sarah and Captain Konig looked at him in bewilderment.

The following morning, Sarah and Jack rode over to the little church at Hallerton. Through the trees they could see a wagon being unloaded. Jack's telescope revealed that it was William Kemble and the Gallants.

"You can hear that tenor bell nearly a mile out at sea," Jack whispered, giving the telescope to Sarah. "Watchtower, signal station and storeroom. The gang fill the pews and the contraband fills the crypt. For what we are about to receive, may the Kembles make us truly thankful!"

"But what about the parson – ?" began Sarah.

"The parson's in their pocket," Jack went on. "He's married to Silas's sister. And she rules him with a rod of iron!"

"We must go to the Excise Officer immediately!" said Sarah, handing back the telescope.

"Go to the sharks?" exclaimed Jack incredulously. "Never!"

"But these men are smugglers!" Sarah looked at him indignantly. "They're cheating the Exchequer of thousands."

"Cheating the Exchequer," mocked Jack. "The boot's on the other foot. The tax on tea is eighty per cent. There's taxes on everything that's pleasant to see, feel or taste. The rich man's spice. The poor man's salt. Even brass nails for the coffins – " He looked at her – "And ribbons for the bride . . ."

Sarah turned away. "So you intend doing nothing to stop it?" she said finally.

"I'm a smuggler, Miss Morton," Jack retorted. "You told me so the first time I met you. And I believe in what I'm doing."

"But the Kembles tried to kill you!"

"So they did, ma'am, but I'll not go to the sharks about it." Jack smiled at her. "That puzzles you, don't it?"

He turned and began walking slowly away from Hallerton. Sarah caught him up and they returned to the Hall in silence. Jack was deep in thought; he had one advantage over the Kembles – they thought he was dead.

At the Hall, Honesty told him that Jacob had installed himself at the cottage and taken over Jack's boat. The smuggler smiled grimly to himself. Jacob would be the first of the Gallants to be dealt with; and Jacob would bring him Silas.

That night, Jack made his way into the Quayhaven caves and climbed the ladder to the secret chamber by his fireplace. Through a small spy-hole he could see Jacob eating at the table while the wind howled eerily round the cottage. Very carefully, he opened the panel and climbed through into the room. He moved silently towards the table, and stopped a little way behind Jacob's chair, half in the shadows, but with his face just lit by the lantern over the table.

"*Jacob!*" he hissed in a long drawn-out whisper.

Jacob was just about to put a piece of mutton in his mouth when he froze. Then very slowly he sat upright and looked uneasily to each side.

"Jacob!" repeated Jack in a ghostly hiss.

Jacob began sweating. His knife dropped from his hand, and then, very slowly, he turned in his chair until he faced Jack. He stared in horror for a moment, and then slowly got to his feet, never taking his eyes off the apparition.

Jack remained standing motionless in the half light while Jacob backed to the door, shaking with fear and breathing heavily. At last his nerve cracked completely and he hurled himself at the door. Flinging it wide with a wail of terror, he stumbled out into the blackness.

Meanwhile, at The Raven Inn, Silas Kemble was holding court. The Gallants sat round him, drinking rum and hanging on his every word.

"Did you ever hear tell of my grandfather and the Customs House at Quayhaven?" he boomed.

It was largely a rhetorical question – most of the Gallants had heard the story many times, but they knew better than to interrupt him.

"He was running 'baccy," Silas continued, puffing away at a long churchwarden pipe.

"Tea," said William.

"Shut up, William," said Silas. "It was 'baccy. Ten tons of hard Cavendish. But the sharks got wind of it and rummaged the sloop. Grandfather got away, but they put the tobacco in the Customs House at Quayhaven." Silas paused for dramatic effect. "But it weren't there for long."

"That it weren't," said William.

Silas gave his brother a dirty look. "Grand-dad attacked the place with thirty men. Took the tobacco and left eight dead sharks behind him. Now that's the way to do it, boys. A proper job, eh?"

There was a roar from the Gallants, who slapped their thighs and stamped their feet on the floor of the taproom in approval. During the applause, William suddenly caught sight of Honesty standing at the edge of the group. He leaped up and grabbed the boy, almost throttling him.

"*William*!" shouted Silas sharply.

William, rather reluctantly, let Honesty go.

"I've kept my mouth shut, Mister Kemble, I have,"

whined Honesty. "I haven't said a word to anyone, see? I'd hardly come here if I had, would I?"

Silas eyed him suspiciously. "Why have you come?" he said mildly.

Honesty puffed out his chest importantly.

"Could we talk private-like?"

Silas laughed at Honesty's impudence. "Private? If you've anything to say, my little Welsh rabbit, you'd better say it now."

Honesty leaned forward and whispered in Silas's ear. "I know where you can find Mister Jack's stuff. All of it."

Honesty took a packet of tobacco from his pocket and put it on the table. William whipped it open with his knife and sniffed at it.

"Best leaf," he said.

"There's boxes by the hundred, and enough brandy to float a frigate," said Honesty. "Bales of cloth, lace, boxes of tea – "

"Where?" growled Silas.

Honesty looked at him craftily. "Well now, you'd have to cut me in!" he whispered.

William grabbed him again and shook him like a rat. "Cut you in?" he said savagely. "I'll cut you up, you shab-rag!"

Silas remained calm. "If you're telling me lies, I'll fry you for supper!" he told the boy.

Honesty looked hard at him. "I never tell lies," he said.

Silas patted him on the head. "Then you'll have your share," he chuckled.

The thought of laying his hands on Jack Vincent's contraband excited Silas's greedy heart, and he ordered his men to prepare. The Gallants were on their feet, checking pistols and pulling on topcoats, when suddenly the door was thrown open and Jacob staggered in, wild-eyed and trembling: everyone stared at him.

38

"What's up, Jacob?" asked Silas, looking at him curiously.

Jacob turned to one of the serving girls. "Fetch me some rum," he said hoarsely.

"You're as white as a ghost!" tittered William.

Jacob swung round. "Stow it!" he shouted.

The serving girl brought Jacob his rum and he downed it at a gulp. The Gallants were puzzled. Jacob caught sight of Honesty. "So you caught him," he breathed.

Silas nodded. "One of us now – ain't you, Welshy? He's going to lead us to Jack Vincent's hoard."

At the mention of this name, Jacob shuddered visibly.

"Cheerly, man – you'll get your share," said Silas with a grin.

"I don't want it!" Jacob said savagely. "Or that cursed cottage!"

"And why's that, pray?" asked Silas, sensing that something was very wrong.

Jacob licked his lips. "I've seen him!"

"Seen who?"

"Jack Vincent!" Jacob burst out.

The Gallants, all superstitious men, began murmuring among themselves.

"Staring, he was," Jacob breathed. "Staring at me from the shadows. He's come back from hell, I tell you!"

The men stared at Jacob as if transfixed, but Silas was quick to break the spell. He was a hard-headed man, and nothing frightened him. He took the glass from Jacob's hand and held it up in front of the man's face.

"That's the only spirit you've seen tonight, Jacob!" he jeered. "And a sight too much of it, I reckon. Stay here then. There'll be more for the rest of us." He turned to Honesty. "Eh, my little smuggler?"

Honesty nodded and, having thus rallied his men, Silas

led them away from The Raven, leaving Jacob still trembling at the memory of what he had seen in the cottage.

Carrying torches, Silas and the Gallants followed Honesty to the mouth of a cave in a rocky promontory to the west of Quayhaven.

"What's your game, Welshy?" grated Silas suspiciously. "The sharks search these caves regular as clockwork. Only a fool would use them."

"Maybe so, Mister Kemble," Honesty replied. "But the stuff's in there – I know it is."

"You'd better be telling the truth," warned Silas as the gang went into the cave.

They reached the main chamber and by the light of their torches could see a pile of boxes stacked on a shelf of rock. Silas's practised eye quickly totted up their possible worth. It was a healthy sum. He turned to Honesty.

"I was just beginning to doubt you, Welshy!" he chuckled.

"Where's the rest of it!" snarled William.

"Further in," Honesty replied.

William scrambled forward to the ledge. His hand touched the boxes –

"Silas!" It was Jack's voice, echoing eerily round the cave. William jumped back as if he had been stung.

"What the devil – !" cursed Silas.

"Silas Kemble!" wailed the voice.

Honesty appeared to be terrified. "That's Mister Jack!" he stammered. "But he's dead! He's dead!"

There was consternation among the Gallants and their eyes darted into every shadow of the cave. Even Silas was beginning to tremble.

"Gull Rock!" sobbed the disembodied voice. "Gull Rock!"

40

A cold sweat broke out on Silas's brow and his body shook. The Gallants stared at their leader; just as terrified.

"You are damned, Silas! And all who follow you! Damned! Damned!"

For a moment longer, the men stood transfixed and then, led by William uttering a howl of fear, they turned and fled. Only Silas held his ground. "Come back you cowards!" he roared.

But the men took not the slightest notice of him; they charged away into the darkness, leaving Silas alone with Honesty.

The boy's torch sent giant shadows flickering round the walls of the cave. Silas drew his cutlass and put it to Honesty's throat.

"He's alive – ain't he, boy? You're no phantom, Vincent!" he called into the darkness. "Show yourself or I'll run the boy through!"

Jack walked forward into the pool of light, with Sarah by his side. Silas grinned and nodded his head.

"Playing the ghost, eh?" he chuckled. "That's an old smuggler's trick!"

"I knew it wouldn't scare you off, Silas," Jack answered. "But I wanted you alone because we have to talk."

Silas was puzzled to see Sarah, a young lady of some standing in the community, with such a well-known smuggler. But talk was the last thing he wanted to do. He ran at Jack and cut down at his head with his cutlass. Had the blow landed, it would have split Jack's skull to his shoulders. But he swayed out of reach and drew his own weapon.

For such a large man, Silas was very light on his feet and his quickness was surprising. The ferocity of his attack forced Jack to give ground, but he defended himself skilfully and soon began getting the measure of his opponent. They circled, each seeking an opening. Silas

41

parried a lightning thrust and tried to lop off Jack's sword arm. The sheer weight of his blows began to beat down Jack's guard. But he grew too confident and, finally, ducking under a savage thrust, Jack stepped in and kicked the big man's legs from under him.

Silas crashed to the ground and shook his head, half-stunned. The point of Jack's cutlass was at his throat.

"If you kill me, Jack boy," he gasped, "you'll never leave here alive."

Jack looked down at him grimly. "I don't want to kill you – you bloodthirsty old tyrant. What good would that do? Now listen – and listen well. I know about the church at Hallerton."

Sarah moved forward. "And so do I," she said.

"One word to the sharks," continued Jack, "and you'll never be able to use it again."

Silas glared venomously at Jack. "I'll have you killed," he whispered.

"And lose the church?" Jack mocked.

Silas glanced at Sarah.

"No Silas," Jack said calmly. "You wouldn't have *her* killed. Captain Konig's grand-daughter? It wouldn't be the militia then, Silas. It'd be a regiment of dragoons. And your days would be numbered."

There was a long silence in the cave. Silas got to his feet slowly. Vincent had bested him and he knew it.

"You keep out of my way," continued Jack coolly, "and I'll keep out of yours."

"A truce then," muttered Silas.

"Yes, a truce. And one thing more! Mr Cooper gets his silk back." Silas had to agree; unless he did as Jack asked, the Hallerton church would be raided by the Customs men. Without another word, he turned on his heel and strode out of the cave.

"It won't end there," warned Sarah.

"I know," said Jack. "But I've got him rattled, and he'll think twice before tackling me again." He turned to Honesty. "Now let's get this stuff back to my cave before the sharks find it!"

CHAPTER THREE

HONESTY attached himself to Jack just as a stray dog might
have done, and the smuggler hadn't the heart to tell him
that he really preferred to be alone. But the boy had saved
his life and Jack would never forget it. So he let him sleep
in the shed at the side of the cottage, and he came and
went as he pleased. Sometimes he ate with Jack, but often
he would hang around Westmore Hall, doing odd jobs for
Captain Konig and Sarah.

The captain began to get him interested in ships and
the sea, and taught him how to use a sextant and read a
chart. He showed him a model of one of his own ships,
and before long Honesty could rattle off the name of every
sail.

As his knowledge grew, Jack found that he was useful
on board the *Mary Jane*. He took him on runs to Guernsey;
to Roscoff and St Malo; ports almost entirely given over
to smuggling.

It was the time of the uneasy peace with France, known
as the Treaty of Amiens. But both nations knew that it was
only a breathing space; sooner or later the war would
flare up once more.

One night, Honesty and Jack descended the iron ladder
from the chamber at the back of the fireplace, carrying
lanterns.

"Where are we off to tonight, then?" asked Honesty.

"Cherbourg," replied Jack laconically.

"Oh, I like Cherbourg," chattered the boy. "Very nice
it is, considering it's foreign. Not like a Frenchy port at
all. More like Swansea."

They reached the bottom of the ladder and set out towards the chamber where Jack kept his equipment and most of his contraband.

"Ever been to Swansea, Mister Jack?"

Jack sighed wearily.

"Best port in the world, Swansea."

They reached Jack's storage cave where barrels and bales were piled up to the roof. The smuggler hung his lantern on an iron hook and began collecting the various things he would need for the journey. Then, with Honesty still chattering behind him, he led the way to the mouth of the cave.

It was a bright, moonlit night as they walked across the beach to where the *Mary Jane* lay hidden in the tiny cove, but suddenly Jack flattened himself against the rocks and extinguished his lantern.

"What is it?" whispered Honesty.

Jack nodded towards the beach, and Honesty peeped round the rocks.

Two sailors were leaning against a long-boat drawn up on the pebbled foreshore. A few yards away from them stood a cloaked figure. He wore the plumed hat of a French naval officer. Honesty ducked back into the shadows.

"Frenchies!" whispered Jack.

A whistle was heard from the cliff-top and the officer returned it. As he stood in the moonlight, looking upwards, a satchel came sailing down to land at his feet, but as he picked it up and began walking back to the boat, Jack leapt out and challenged him.

"You there!" he shouted.

Immediately, the officer drew a pistol from under his cloak and fired at Jack. Fortunately, his aim was poor and the bullet went wide. He threw the pistol at Jack and ran to the long boat. The sailors drew their cutlasses and rushed Jack, who parried their blows and sent one of them sprawling to the ground with a blow from his fist. His companion cut at Jack's head, but he ducked and, with the flat of his cutlass, smacked him across his spine. With a howl of pain, the man stumbled to his knees and dropped his weapon.

Unnerved by Jack's skill, the two sailors scrambled to their feet and made off down the beach.

Jack advanced on the officer, who had also drawn his sword. Their blades crossed in the moonlight, and they fought in silence. But the wet stones of the foreshore proved the Frenchman's undoing, and he slipped on them and tumbled over.

Jack told him to get up, and taking the leather satchel from him, examined its contents.

"What's all them drawings?" said Honesty, holding up the lantern.

"Unless I'm mistaken," answered Jack grimly, "these are plans of the Quayhaven Fort and all the gun emplacements along the coast from here to Farnmouth Castle."

They tied the officer's hands behind him and took him up to the fort. Near the gate they crouched in the darkness and Jack put the leather satchel round the Frenchman's neck. Then he pushed him towards the astonished sentry and watched as he was taken inside the fort. Then he and Honesty hurried back to the cove and put to sea.

"If we'd turned him in, personal-like," complained Honesty, "we might have got a reward."

"We've wasted enough time as it is," Jack replied, and set course for Cherbourg.

"We might even have got a medal," went on Honesty wistfully. "My Uncle, Mostyn, had a lovely string of medals."

"He won them?" queried Jack incredulously.

"Of course he did," grinned Honesty. "Mind you, he was playing with marked cards."

At the fort the following morning, Captain Armstrong – the garrison commander – studied the plans found on the French officer. Mr Marwood, the Customs Officer for the borough, was with him. Marwood was an ambitious man who had worked hard to reach his present position.

"A spy in our very midst, Marwood," exclaimed Captain Armstrong, thumping the papers on his desk. "These documents show every gun, every strong point, and the disposition of every man along this coast! The spy must be caught, Marwood, and quickly!" He poured him a glass of brandy and Marwood took it greedily.

"I trust I can count on your help?" continued the captain.

"I wish I could, Captain," replied Marwood, "but it's out of the question. Smuggling is on the increase, and I must put that first, sir."

"But with your men I could cover the whole coast," said the captain irritably.

"Maybe, sir," said Marwood, "but I've precious few preventative officers as you well know. And none to spare. I would neglect my duty if – "

"Your duty is the safety of England, man!" Armstrong interrupted.

"I'm sorry, Captain," said Marwood stubbornly. "It's not possible."

"I'm disappointed in you, Marwood," sneered the captain, looking at the Customs man down his nose. "Deuced disappointed. I had expected some sort of co-operation."

Marwood flushed. "Co-operation? Two weeks ago I begged for assistance. Not once, not twice, but three times, I asked you to send a party of dragoons to help me catch a gang of smugglers. If you will remember, sir, you told me to apply to the War Office!" Marwood drained his glass and banged it down on the desk. "And what happened when your men did arrive?" he continued. "The smugglers plied them with brandy and tobacco and the dragoons let them get away!"

Captain Armstrong looked coolly at the irate figure before him. Couldn't the fellow control himself?

"Want another drink, Marwood?" he sneered.

At this moment, Sarah was escorted into the room by a lieutenant. It was typical that none of the officers at the fort were able to interrogate the French officer in his own tongue – and he refused to speak English. Sarah, who spoke French fluently, had been asked if she would question him. It was all very embarrassing for Captain Armstrong.

"Ah, Miss Morton," he said, as Sarah entered. "You know Marwood, our Customs fellow, don't you?"

Sarah nodded coolly. She knew Mr Marwood very well indeed. On several occasions, he had asked her to marry him, but she had made it quite clear she wasn't interested. "Good morning, sir," she said.

Marwood blushed. "Sarah . . . er . . . Miss Morton. This is an unexpected pleasure."

The French officer was brought in but he refused to answer any of Sarah's questions. Instead, he smiled at her, paid her a series of extravagant compliments and finally took her hand and kissed it. Sarah thought he was charming.

"Damned Froggie!" swore Armstrong as the prisoner was taken back to his cell. "I regret your time has been so wasted."

Marwood stepped forward. "Might I escort you to your carriage?" he asked.

"As you wish, sir," replied Sarah coldly.

As they crossed the courtyard to where Captain Konig

49

sat in the open carriage, Marwood said to Sarah, "I regret our last meeting ended so stormily."

"I had forgotten it already, Mr Marwood," Sarah replied.

"I have not," persisted Marwood. "Nor the cause of the dispute."

"If you mean Mr Vincent," said Sarah angrily, "I must tell you that I will not be dictated to in the matter of my acquaintances."

"But the man is a smuggler!"

"Is he, Mr Marwood?" retorted Sarah.

They had reached the carriage. Marwood bowed politely. "Good afternoon, Mr Konig, sir," he said ingratiatingly. "The Frenchman refuses to talk."

Captain Konig chuckled. "He must be a brave man to resist Sarah!"

Marwood helped her into the carriage.

"I hope to see you at Westmore Hall again, Mr Marwood," said Captain Konig.

"That rather depends on your grand-daughter, sir," Marwood replied, looking fondly at Sarah.

"I'm sure she'll be delighted to see you," said the Captain.

Sarah glared at her grandfather and drove the carriage out through the main gates of the fort without so much as a backward glance at the wretched Customs Officer.

Later the following day, Jack and Honesty returned from the run to Cherbourg and found Silas and William Kemble sitting comfortably in the cottage, warming themselves by a blazing fire.

"How was the trip?" asked Silas, looking round as the door opened. "Profitable?"

Jack looked at him steadily. "I thought we agreed to keep out of each other's way, Kemble," he said quietly.

Silas chuckled. "That we did, Jack. But now that deal's off. Thought I might try offering you a partnership."

"After trying to kill me," Jack replied.

Silas laughed loudly, and William sniggered. "You're a hard man to kill," Silas went on. "So I'm asking you, nicely, if you wouldn't like to come alongside. A bit of co-operation, that's what I'm after."

"Why?"

Silas chuckled. "Because it's a better way of workin' to my mind. You keep the trade you won away from us, and operate under our protection."

"And what do you get out of it?" asked Jack suspiciously

Silas shrugged. "Well, you'll have to up your prices. Charge what we do. That way you can give us half what you make and still show the same profit!"

Jack flung open the door. "*Get out!*"

William stood up and swaggered over to him. "You're not in the navy now!" he mocked.

In a sudden rage, Jack grabbed him by the coat, swung him round and slammed him against the wall.

Silas heaved himself out of the chair. "All right, Jack boy," he said. "No need to lose your temper. We're going. But remember, we asked you nice."

The two Kembles disappeared into the darkness and Jack slammed the door with an oath.

Late that night, Honesty was given his orders. He was to deliver a tub of brandy to a nearby farm, take some tobacco to an old fisherman, and finally leave a bale of silk outside Westmore Hall. On no account was he to go inside, and Jack warned him that if he heard that anything had been stolen, he would kick him into the sea. Honesty was most indignant.

"I never steal from friends, Mister Jack!" said Honesty indignantly.

"I doubt if you've got any," Jack replied. "Now on your way!"

Honesty loaded his cart and then poked his head in through the door. "By the way," he said, "If the Kembles do away with you before I get back – can I have your telescope?"

CHAPTER FOUR

WESTMORE HALL was in darkness when Honesty crept silently across the courtyard and placed Jack's present against the back door. He was surprised when the weight of the bale pushed the door slowly inwards. It was unlike Captain Konig to be so careless, thought Honesty. Perhaps something was wrong! He slipped inside.

As he tiptoed slowly down the passage, he heard someone cough in the library: he peered round the open door.

Two men crouched in the fireplace, and as Honesty watched, one of them was seized with a rasping cough. In his eagerness to find out what they were up to, Honesty tripped against a stool and it clattered to the floor. The men swung round as he ducked away from the door and fled down the passage.

He raced out into the yard, vaulted the gate and sped on across the open moor. His life in the Bristol docks had been one of constant pursuit and he could run like a hare. When he was sure that no-one was following, he slackened his pace and began to take stock; the men at Westmore Hall were thieves, but if anything was missing he would be blamed for it: it was important that he should tell Mister Jack everything.

But in his excitement, he over-dramatised what had happened so much that Jack was convinced he was lying.

"I looked them straight in the eye," Honesty told him, "and they was off like frightened rabbits."

"Did they take anything?" asked Jack.

"I dunno. I don't think so."

53

"Would you know 'em again?"

"I doubt it," said Honesty.

"You said you looked 'em straight in the eye!" Jack reminded him. "You just can't stop lying, can you?"

"I'm telling you the truth!" retorted Honesty. "They – they was wearing masks. The eyes was all I *could* see."

"I've stood your lying long enough!" said Jack. "Out!"

"Would I lie to you?" said Honesty.

Jack advanced on the boy and threw him out of the cottage by the scruff of his neck. Honesty picked himself up angrily.

"It's the truth!" he shouted at Jack, and then ran off into the darkness.

He made his way gloomily to an old barn on the edge of the moor. Here, he curled up in the warm straw and after cursing Jack heartily in Welsh, fell instantly asleep.

He awoke to find William Kemble bending over him with a pistol in his hand.

"We wants words with you, Honesty Evans!" he snarled.

At about this time, Sarah Morton found the little bale of silk in the hall, and she was already planning the dress she intended to make with it, when a thunderous knocking was heard at the main door.

She opened it to find Captain Armstrong outside with two dragoons.

"I apologise for this intrusion," said Armstrong stiffly. "But I must speak with your grandfather, ma'am. It is a matter of the greatest urgency."

With a frown, Sarah stepped back into the hallway and led the captain and his men to the library. Captain Konig rose with a bewildered air.

"I'll come straight to the point, Captain Konig," said Armstrong. "This morning I received a letter naming you as the man we seek."

"But that's ridiculous!" exclaimed Sarah, drawing close to her grandfather.

"Quite so, ma'am," replied Armstrong gravely. "Captain Konig has always seemed to me a man of the highest honour. Nevertheless, we must humbly ask permission to search the house."

"Who wrote this letter?" Sarah continued angrily.

"It was not signed –"

"And you believe some anonymous scrawl worthy of consideration?"

Captain Konig put his hand on Sarah's arm. "We have nothing to hide, Sarah, and the captain must do his duty."

Armstrong bowed. "My humblest apologies, sir," he said. "But you understand my position."

Taking a bayonet from one of the dragoons, who all this while had stood stiffly to attention, Armstrong went to the fireplace and began feeling into the darkness with its point. He dislodged a small wooden box from a ledge inside the chimney and it fell with a clatter into the grate. Armstrong picked it up and brought it over to Captain Konig's desk.

"Have you seen this before, sir?" he asked evenly.

"Why certainly," replied the astonished Captain Konig. "I keep my correspondence in it, but I assure you its place is on my desk not up the chimney!"

Armstrong forced the box open with his bayonet. Inside it were some papers; drawings of the fort and of the coastal defences.

"Strange correspondence, sir," said Armstrong coldly to the captain. "These drawings are identical to those found on the Frenchman."

"But this . . . this is none of my doing!" gasped Captain Konig.

"My grandfather has no reason to betray this country!" said Sarah angrily.

Armstrong scooped a handful of gold coins from the

box and showed them to her: they were French. "This could be the reason," he said coldly. He turned again to Captain Konig. "England welcomed you," he said, giving the old man a look of withering contempt, "is this how you repay her?" He nodded to his men and Captain Konig was marched outside. Here he was manacled despite Sarah's protests and bundled into Armstrong's carriage. Armstrong bowed stiffly to the distraught girl, climbed in beside his prisoner and drove off.

Jack was sitting on the doorstep of his cottage in the afternoon sunlight, mending one of his nets, when Sarah galloped up. With tears in her eyes, she told him how Armstrong had found the box hidden in the fireplace and arrested her grandfather as a spy.

Jack got to his feet, remembering Honesty's story, and his expression hardened. Someone was deliberately trying to blacken Captain Konig's good name.

"They put chains on his wrists," sobbed Sarah. "His face was so white. I tried to – "

"Did you see this letter?" Jack asked.

"*No, I didn't see the letter!*" Sarah blazed at him. "It's all lies anyway! Grandfather is innocent – you know he is! If you think for a moment that he could betray – "

"Don't be foolish, Sarah," Jack cut in. "Honesty brought that silk to the Hall last night. There were two men in the library."

"Why didn't you tell me this before?" said Sarah angrily.

"Because I didn't believe him."

"I must tell Captain Armstrong," said Sarah.

Jack shook his head. "No," he said. "Not Armstrong."

"You surely can't think he – " Sarah began.

"You didn't see the letter, did you?"

Sarah stared at him. "But that's absurd! – Captain Armstrong's the garrison commander!"

"And in charge of the coastal defences," Jack went on. "With all the maps and plans of the fort."

"That's ridiculous!" said Sarah.

Jack nodded. "Perhaps. But don't say anything to him at the moment," he warned.

"Is that all you can say?" she cried. "Is that all the help you can give me?"

"Yes," said Jack calmly. "For the present."

"Then, damn you, Jack Vincent!" she cursed, remounting her horse, and galloped away along the cliff path.

Jack watched her go. He understood her anger. He shared her quick temper and lack of caution. It had landed him in trouble three years ago at his Court of Inquiry. But he knew that if Armstrong was behind a plot to ruin Captain Konig, a chance word could put him on his guard and spoil the kindly old man's chances of eventual release.

"Mr Vincent!" rasped a voice.

Jack spun round and saw one of Silas Kemble's Gallants pushing his way through the bushes leading Honesty, who was bound and gagged. It was Giles Sawney, and he leered at Jack.

"I've been told to bring this littl'un back," he said, pushing Honesty to the ground. "But we've taken your boat."

Jack took an angry step towards Sawney, and the man backed away.

"It's no use trying to find out where we've taken her, Jack boy," he laughed nervously. "You'd better throw in with them or she'll be scuppered." Sawney gave a curious rasping cough. "You've got till next high tide to make up your mind."

He turned and began shambling away down the cliff path, his laughter once again turning to a cough. Jack kneeled by Honesty and untied him.

57

"I couldn't stop 'em, Mister Jack," the boy gasped. "Honest I couldn't. They'd have killed me!"

"It's all right, boy," Jack reassured him. "I know their ways – "

"Thanks, Mister Jack," said Honesty gratefully.

Jack helped him to his feet. "I owe you an apology," he said.

Honesty's eyes widened. "An apology? How so?"

"I didn't believe your story," Jack explained. "But I do now."

"You do?" Honesty was clearly delighted.

"Are you sure you wouldn't recognise those two men?"

Honesty frowned. "No – except – one of them might have been the man who brought me here. I recognised his cough."

"Giles Sawney, eh?" murmured Jack. "Well I know where to find him. He'll be on his way to the 'Admiral Drake' down in Quayhaven."

The Admiral Drake was a sleazy tavern opposite the harbour wall. It was frequented by fishermen, and soldiers from the garrison. A place where fights were the order of the day and drunkenness abounded. Smoke-filled and noisy, it smelled of stale tobacco, beer and rotting fish.

When Jack and Honesty reached it, they found Giles Sawney in the far corner drinking and laughing with one of his mates. They walked up to the table unnoticed and then, just as Sawney began his familiar cough, Jack tapped him on the shoulder.

"That's a nasty cough," he murmured calmly. "Did you catch it at Westmore Hall?"

Sawney glared up at him. "What are you talking about?" he snarled.

"I saw you there!" joined in Honesty.

"You prove it!" shouted Sawney, and drew his cutlass. In one swift movement, Jack tipped up the table and sent Sawney staggering back, but his mate sprang at him and tried to brain him with a bottle. Jack swayed sideways and caught the man on the chin with a punch that would have done credit to a professional prize-fighter. The man collapsed in a heap and Jack swung back to find Sawney holding Honesty in front of him with the blade of his cutlass across the boy's neck.

"Keep back, Vincent," he warned, dragging Honesty to the door. "Or I'll do for him, I promise you!"

Jack hesitated, and Sawney flung Honesty to the floor and ran from the tavern. The boy scrambled up, and Jack had to push him aside as he raced out after Sawney.

The two of them raced along the harbour wall, with Jack gaining on Sawney at every yard. Finally, the smuggler turned at bay and the fight was on.

"Who paid you to plant the evidence on Konig, Sawney?" asked Jack calmly as he parried the wild swipes of the frightened Gallant. With a flick of his wrist, he sent Sawney's weapon flying through the air to disappear into the sea.

"Who was it?" he repeated, with his cutlass at Sawney's throat.

"Silas! It was Silas, damn you!" gasped Sawney hoarsely.

Meanwhile, Sarah had gone to the fort to tell her grandfather about the men Honesty had seen in the library. But she remembered Jack's warning, and kept this information from Armstrong.

"I shall find the man who put you here," she told her grandfather, "and I shall bring him to justice!"

"And I forbid you to do anything," said Captain Konig. "This is a dangerous business, Sarah."

"Try to stop me!" she retorted.

Captain Konig looked at her with a sad smile.

"You are so like your mother," he said softly. "She was

just as headstrong at your age; and so determined to marry John Morton."

"Did you object to that?" asked Sarah.

Captain Konig shook his head. "No. John was a fine man. The best of my captains." He paused and his eyes had a faraway look in them. "I remember the day you were born. He put you in my arms for a moment, and looked at me with such a strange look: almost as if he could see into the future and was saying, 'look after her well'."

There was a long silence, and Sarah could see the tears in her grandfather's eyes. "It was only a year before the sea claimed both of them," he said in little more than a whisper.

Sarah knelt down and took his hands in hers. "But I'm still with you," she said quietly. "And intend to secure your release from this prison. Have courage, Grandfather!"

Captain Konig looked into her eyes and smiled. "You are right, child," he said. "We must never give up hope!"

CHAPTER FIVE

EARLY the next morning, Mr Marwood galloped into the courtyard of Westmore Hall just as Sarah was leading her horse from the stables.

"I cannot believe this terrible accusation against your grandfather," he said. "And whatever the outcome of his trial, I'll never believe him guilty."

The warmth and directness of Marwood's speech made Sarah feel somewhat ashamed that she had treated the man so badly in the past.

"Nothing will alter my high opinion of him," continued Marwood. "Or my deep regard for you. And though you may think me indelicate to pursue matters of the heart at such a time – "

Sarah attempted to interrupt him, but Marwood would not be silenced. "Here me out, please," he continued. "If Captain Konig is found guilty, which is not impossible, society will turn its back on you. You will be alone. Now I realise, ma'am, that my position as Customs Officer is not of sufficient standing, but I had hoped that you might consider me as a man to whom you could turn if such a dreadful circumstance were to come about."

At that moment, they saw Jack walking across the garden towards them.

"I want to talk to you, Sarah," called Jack. He looked at Marwood. "Alone."

Marwood was furious, but Sarah welcomed the interruption.

"Will you excuse me, Mr Marwood?" she said politely. "Perhaps you could wait for me in the library."

Marwood managed to control his anger, bowed and went into the house.

"Well, what do you want?" Sarah asked Jack.

He told her how Giles Sawney had planted the evidence on orders from the Kembles. Sarah reasoned that if the Kembles were responsible, Jack's suspicions of Armstrong were groundless. But he still couldn't believe the Kembles could have obtained plans of the fort and other coastal defences by themselves. There had to be someone behind them and so he told Sarah to be patient. Besides, they had his boat and he didn't intend to let them sink her. Sarah was furious.

"That boat means more to you than my grandfather's life, does it?" she retorted. "It's plain that if I wait for *you* to bring the Kembles to justice, they'll die of old age!"

She turned and ran to the house, slamming the door in Jack's face as he tried to follow her.

Marwood was surprised when Sarah came storming into the library.

"If I spoke out of turn, Miss Morton," he said hastily, "I beg you to forgive me."

He blinked in astonishment as she took two small pistols from a drawer in her grandfather's desk.

"You will excuse me, Mr Marwood," Sarah replied. "But I have pressing business elsewhere!"

As she brushed past Jack in the hallway, completely ignoring him, he saw the pistols and ran after her. Out in the courtyard, Sarah was already spurring her horse away from the Hall, so Jack leapt on Marwood's stallion and galloped after her as the wretched Customs Officer came stumbling out of the house and shouted angrily after him.

Jack knew that Sarah meant to confront the Kembles. In her present mood she was angry enough to shoot them both. He cursed her wild spirit as he chased after her.

Women and firearms did not mix. Besides, he doubted if she'd ever fired a pistol in her life.

He yelled at her to stop, but she didn't even look back at him. They were on the cliff path, with the rocks and the foaming white sea two hundred feet below them. If either horse stumbled, they would both plummet to their deaths.

Leaning forward in the saddle, Jack tried to snatch her horse's bridle. Sarah lashed at him with her crop and forced him to drop back. Coming alongside her again, he launched himself from the saddle and the two of them crashed to the ground. They rolled over and over, slithering dangerously near the cliff edge. Below them, the waves crashed thunderously on the needle-sharp rocks.

"Lie still, or we'll both go over," Jack warned her. Then he grabbed the riding crop from her hand and threw it into the sea. Ripping open her riding jacket he pulled out the pistols and stood up.

Sarah got angrily to her feet. "I'd have made the Kembles talk if you hadn't stopped me!"

"Don't be a fool!" Jack replied angrily.

Sarah's eyes blazed into his. "Are you afraid of action?"

Jack's answer to this was to throw away the pistols, take her in his arms and kiss her. Sarah kicked him hard on the shins and then, as he let her go, she gave him a stinging blow across the face.

Jack grinned at her and rubbed his cheek. "You said you wanted action," he chuckled. "Leave the Kembles to me!"

That night, The Raven was crowded. Silas sat with brother William, swapping tales of past smuggling feats with the Gallants. The ordinary folk of Quayhaven kept away from them; none of them trusted Silas.

Suddenly, the door was kicked open and Jack stood in the doorway, a pistol in his hand.

Silas waved cheerfully. "Evenin' Vincent," he chuckled.

"You'll find that door opens easier if you turn the handle."

William downed a tankard of ale. "Come to join us have you?" he leered.

"I've come for information," Jack replied.

"Want to know where your boat is, do you?" asked Silas. "You come in here, waving a pistol, and expect to frighten me and the lads. It'd take more than that popgun!"

There was a roar of laughter from the Gallants, but when Honesty appeared and handed Jack a blunderbuss the laughter died away. If Jack fired the fearsome weapon, it could put paid to quite a few of them.

Jack smiled at their consternation. "Now, I want to know why you've turned traitor, Kemble," he said loudly for the benefit of everyone there. "Why have you been helping the French?"

Silas stirred uneasily. "What d'you mean, Vincent?" he growled.

"Who gave you the documents to incriminate Captain Konig?" continued Jack loudly.

The crowd began murmuring among themselves.

"Sawney told us everything," chipped in Honesty. "So don't try to deny it. You've been helping the French spy!"

All eyes were on Silas Kemble. He wiped the sweat from his brow and licked his lips.

"It's all lies. You're bluffing, Vincent." He turned to the Gallants. "He's bluffing, lads!"

Jack stared at Silas remorselessly. His finger tightened on the trigger of the blunderbuss. "Who's the French spy, Silas?" he continued.

One of the Gallants stood up. It was old Benjamin, the fisherman who had captured Honesty the day Jack had been taken to Gull Rock. "We've always been loyal to you, Kemble," he said. "But this is different. We may be smugglers, but we're loyal to England first and foremost! Ain't that so, lads?"

There was a chorus of agreement, and Jack waved the Gallants away from the two Kembles who now found themselves alone.

"I'm still waiting," grated Jack. "Who is he, Silas?"

"Do for 'em, Vincent," roared another of the Gallants. "Send 'em to hell, where they belong!"

William's nerve cracked first. He leapt to his feet, cowering away from the blunderbuss. "It's Marwood. Marwood's the spy!" he screamed in terror.

"Marwood!" gasped Honesty.

"He tells us when and where to expect his patrols," gabbled William feverishly. "We have to do him favours in return."

"And put all England at risk!" said Jack furiously. "Now I want proof." He raised the blunderbuss and pointed it directly at William.

"All right! All right," he sobbed. "Molliston Bay, at sunrise tomorrow. He told us to keep away. You'll find him there if you've a mind to. Put that damned gun down!"

"Out of the way, the rest of you!" Jack commanded.

The villagers and Gallants ducked for cover, hiding under the tables and behind the chairs.

"No, Vincent!" screamed William, falling to his knees. "Don't shoot!"

The blunderbuss roared like a cannon and a cloud of soot enveloped both Kembles from head to foot. After a moment's stupefied silence, the entire taproom exploded into laughter. Jack had achieved his aim. Not only had he discovered the spy's identity – he had totally discredited the Kembles, finally making them a laughing-stock.

At dawn, Jack crouched among the rocks in Molliston Bay and watched Marwood receiving payment for his

66

treachery. The man waved as the French long-boat put out to sea, then he walked slowly up the beach.

At the foot of the cliff path, a jumble of rocks marked the transition from cliff to sand; and here Jack confronted him.

"How much did they pay you, Marwood?" he said quietly, stepping from his hiding place, his cutlass in his hand.

Marwood stared at him.

"Or perhaps you do it for love," Jack continued bitterly. The Customs Officer snatched a pistol from under his cloak and fired. The ball caught Jack in the shoulder and its force spun him round and sent him crashing back against the rocks. His cutlass fell from his nerveless fingers.

Marwood put the smoking pistol into his belt and drawing his own sword, advanced on Jack.

"Did you get a bonus for destroying Captain Konig's reputation?" said Jack, wincing with pain.

"It may please you to know that I did," replied Marwood. "I wasn't good enough for Sarah. But the money I've made out of this little venture will alter that!"

"You're finished, you fool!" said Jack evenly.

Marwood lunged at him, and Jack moved like lightning. Swaying out of range, he picked up his cutlass and defended himself left-handed.

Marwood advanced relentlessly, cutting and slashing with unexpected ferocity. Jack retreated up the cliff path, parrying the blows as best he could but unable to return them. He was losing blood, and growing weaker every second. He continued to retreat until they reached the top of the cliff. Here, Marwood made one final attack, driving Jack to the very edge. Then he drew his sword back for the *coup de grâce*. With a shudder of pain, Jack hooked his wounded arm round the man's throat and threw himself to the ground, pulling Marwood over his body. With a yell of terror, Marwood disappeared over the cliff, and plummeted to the rocks below.

Jack staggered to his feet, Marwood's dying scream still echoing inside his head, then he crumpled at the knees as sea and sky swam round him and he lost consciousness.

A patrol of soldiers found him and took him back to the fort. After his wound had been bound up, he was brought before Captain Armstrong, where he told his story.

Captain Armstrong listened in silence. Then he shook his head ruefully. "I never thought that Marwood was the spy," he said. "He visited this fort many times. I thought he came for the brandy."

"Then you'll release Captain Konig?" asked Jack.

"I have already given orders to that effect," replied Captain Armstrong. "You're not the first to accuse Marwood, Mr Vincent."

The door to the ante-chamber opened, and Silas and William Kemble were brought in.

"These two . . . er . . . gentlemen have already told me everything," said the Captain, while Silas grinned nervously.

It was true. Hoping to avoid punishment for their part in the affair, Silas and William had turned against Marwood and revealed he was spying for the French. But if they hoped for a reward they were to be disappointed. Because they had proved themselves such loyal servants of the King, Armstrong told them that he would give them a further opportunity to serve him. He ordered them to join the navy.

William and Silas were dumbfounded. "No, Captain Armstrong – not the navy!" William pleaded.

"I'd rather go to prison," groaned Silas.

Life was grim for the ordinary seaman of those days. Naval discipline was severe and punishments were frequent. To serve a prison sentence was a far more lenient punishment than to serve on a man-of-war. It would be many years before the Kembles came back to Quayhaven. And if they did, they would hardly be welcome. For though smuggling was a way of life for most of the fishermen in the borough, they had no time for traitors.

CHAPTER SIX

AFTER a long search, Jack and Honesty found the *Mary Jane* under a covering of brushwood amid the rushes on the mudflats behind Hallerton. Using rollers, and helped by several farmworkers, they dragged her to the little creek which led down to the sea. Here, they repaired her broken mast and re-rigged the sails. Then they took her round the headland to moor her safely in the tiny cove below Jack's cottage.

Life began to resume a more customary, but still dangerous pattern. A new Customs Officer was appointed. Marwood's replacement was an ambitious man named Taggart, who was keen to make a name for himself. He seemed especially anxious to catch Jack Vincent, and several times his vigilance prevented Jack from making a profitable run. Most of the local smugglers were also suffering because of Taggart's zeal.

One moonlight night, Honesty was walking down a lonely path through a wood, his hands in his pockets and whistling as if he hadn't a care in the world. But as he strode along his eyes darted from side to side, and he caught sight of Taggart and his men watching from the bushes. He pretended not to notice them and walked on, still whistling. Some way ahead Jack was waiting for him.

"The place is crawling with Taggart and his men," reported Honesty.

"Damn his vigilance!" swore Jack softly.

"What do we do now?" asked Honesty anxiously.

Jack shrugged. "Turn back," he said.

"We can't do that!" argued Honesty. "We've got to get

to Farnmouth. Mr Rook's expecting his brandy tonight. Proper livid he'll be."

A cart was heard approaching, and the two of them took cover in the bushes. Through the branches they could see an old man pulling a handcart along the path.

"Who is it?" whispered Honesty.

"Looks like Old Rummy," Jack replied. "I hope for his sake he's abroad on lawful business. Come on – we're going home!"

Old Rummy, breathing heavily, eventually reached Taggart's ambush, and much to his alarm, suddenly found himself surrounded. A lantern was shone into his face. A pleasant, craggy face like an old map. His little eyes twinkled mischievously and darted round his captors like those of a trapped animal.

The tall, lean figure of Mr Taggart stepped forward.

"Well, well!" he smiled. "Rummy Culbert." He turned to his men. "Search the cart!"

Taggart's men moved forward and began stripping the canvas off Rummy's cart. Taggart unsheathed his sword and stabbed at the bales. Then he sniffed. "Smells like tobacco," he said slowly.

"You have a professional nose, sir," replied Rummy deferentially. "Sixty-four pounds of Negrohead I got there. Found it washed up I did. So I says to Mam, my missus, 'As a law-abiding man, I got to turn this lot in.' 'No, no!' she says. 'They'll catch you with it and think you're smuggling again!' "

Taggart nodded sympathetically. He had heard stories like this before.

" 'No, no!' says I to her," Rummy continued dramatically. " 'that Mister Taggart knows I retired long ago! Besides, he can tell when a man's lying and when he's telling the truth!' "

71

"I think I can, Rummy," laughed Taggart. "And you're lying."

The men grabbed Rummy and the old man clutched at his heart.

"Don't tell me I've misjudged you, sir," he groaned

Taggart gave a grim smile. "Oh, no, Rummy!" he said. "I think we understand each other very well."

Taggart took Rummy to his office in the Customs House at Quayhaven. He had the old man put in chains and made him sit on a rickety, three-legged stool in front of him.

"If I bring charges, Rummy, it'll be transportation for you this time," threatened Taggart.

Rummy looked at him craftily. "You said 'if', sir," he said with a wink. "Does that mean you might not?"

Taggart leaned forward over his desk. "I have a proposition to put to you," he said softly.

But before Rummy learnt what the proposition was, the door was flung open and Nan Culbert – Rummy's wife – swept in like a three-masted schooner.

She was a large, damp lady, red-faced and crumpled-looking. Enveloping Rummy in her ample arms, she wailed, "Rummy! What have they done to you?"

"Brought me low, they have," replied Rummy in muffled tones.

Nan released the little man, who was in imminent danger of suffocation, and advanced threateningly on Mr Taggart. "Would you hasten his end, sir?" she wailed. "He's deathly sick. Let him hear your cough, Rummy," she commanded.

Rummy coughed obligingly.

"D'you hear that, sir?" continued Nan. "That's the sound of a man with one foot in the grave. Listen to his chest."

"I'd rather not," replied Taggart, not at all sure how to cope with the frantic virago before him.

"It's like the gurgling of a millpond," sobbed Nan. "The doctor told 'im he had but three months to live. And that were two year ago." She flung herself on her knees and the little office shook. "Set 'im free, sir, I beg you. Then he can end his days at peace in my arms."

Taggart stood up. "I could let him go, Mrs Culbert. But at a price."

"We got no money, Mr Taggart," replied Rummy quickly. "It were all spent on that tobacco."

Taggart shook his head. "It's not money I want, Rummy."

"What then?"

"Jack Vincent!"

Rummy stared at him. Taggart was offering him his freedom: but at a terrible price.

The following night, while the wind howled loudly round his cottage, Jack sat with a coastal chart spread out in front of him and showed Honesty the only part of the coast the Customs officers never bothered to patrol.

"The current's treacherous and the rocks are like razors," Jack told the boy.

"I don't like the look of it," said Honesty.

"That's why it's called the Graveyard," replied Jack.

There was a sudden knocking at the door.

"Who is it?" asked Jack, taking up his pistol. There was no reply, and so he silently slid back the bolt and pulled open the door.

Rummy almost fell into his arms. The old man looked terrible and his breath rattled noisily in his throat.

"Let me sit awhile by your fire, Mr Vincent," he wheezed.

Jack helped him over to the fire. The old man was shivering with cold, and rubbed his arms to warm himself.

"Been at sea fifteen hours," he gasped. "I couldn't bring the stuff ashore on account of the patrols." He coughed

73

painfully. "Then I come over queer and dumped it overboard. Sixty-four pounds of Negrohead tobacco, just waiting to be picked up."

Jack brought him a glass of brandy, and Rummy swallowed it at a gulp and held the glass up for a refill.

"Half of that tobacco is yours," he said, "if you can get it ashore and sell it for me. I ain't got the strength to do it for meself."

"Why come to me?" asked Jack.

Rummy smiled. "Because you're the only man I know who won't cheat me out of the lot," he replied. "You'll play fair, I know you will."

Jack put the chart in front of him. "Show me where you dumped it," he said.

Rummy scanned the chart for a moment, and then pointed. "Half a mile off Foreland Head," he gasped. "My old woman said I was too old for moonraking, and I reckon she was right."

"You're never too old for a bit of mischief," said Honesty in an attempt to cheer him up. "My granny eloped at ninety-three."

Rummy shivered and held out his hands to the fire. "My days of mischief are over, boy," he said. "All I want now is rest and peace and quiet."

Taggart was working late in his office that night when Rummy shuffled in unannounced. "Vincent took the bait," he said with an evil grin.

Taggart slid a bag of coins across the table, and the old man quickly stuffed it inside his ragged coat. Then he shook with a paroxysm of coughing.

"Where's he landing it, Rummy?" Taggart asked.

"The Graveyard," Rummy choked. "He's got it marked on his chart."

"He must be out of his mind!" exclaimed Taggart.

"Only a lunatic would attempt such a landing at this time of year."

Rummy coughed again, his whole body trembling with the violence of the attack. "He can do it," he finally managed to gasp. "I've seen him handle that boat of his." And again he was racked with the tearing cough.

Taggart looked at the old man with concern. "Have a drink, Rummy," he invited kindly.

Rummy shook his head. "I got to get home," he croaked. "I'm feeling very poorly."

The old man tottered to the door and then turned back and looked sadly at the Customs Officer. "How much did they pay Judas, Mr Taggart, sir?" he asked. "Twenty pieces of silver, wasn't it?"

"Thirty," Taggart replied drily. "And then he hanged himself."

"Ay," Rummy nodded. "And I reckon this betrayal will be the death of me."

The door closed behind him and Taggart heard his shuffling steps, accompanied by another coughing fit, dying away in the distance.

It was evening on the following day when Jack steered the *Mary Jane* into the boiling, turbulent waters of the Graveyard.

The place was well named. From a distance the rocks looked like black headstones. Any one of them could rip the bottom out of the *Mary Jane* in a matter of seconds. And in that raging sea, even the finest swimmer would be dashed to pieces.

High on the cliffs, Honesty signalled with a lantern and watched as the frail craft twisted and slid its way through the jagged points of rock. Near him an old pony stood with two large baskets strapped to its sides. Honesty took a coil of rope from one of them and tied one end to the pony's halter. He fastened his lantern to a grappling hook on the other end, and lowered it carefully over the cliff edge.

By now, the *Mary Jane* was safely through the Graveyard and Jack, grateful to be in calmer water, turned her skilfully towards the light swaying a few feet above the waves.

Dangerously close to the cliff, he managed to grab the rope and pull it on board. He took off the lantern, and fastened the grappling hook to a large bundle amidships – a fishing net containing Rummy's kegs of tobacco.

As soon as the 'catch' was secure, Jack gave a tug on the rope and Honesty began leading his pony away from the cliff.

"Here's where you earn your keep, Boney!" he whispered. "Come on! Hup! Hup!"

The bundle bumped its way up the cliff, and Jack turned his lugger and once more threaded his way through the dangerous channel which lead to the open sea.

He sailed round the bay to the *Mary Jane*'s mooring in the cove beneath his cottage, and then hurried back along the cliffs to the spot overlooking the Graveyard. The pony was grazing quietly. Nearby the tobacco was neatly stacked among the bracken. But there was no sign of Honesty.

"*Take him!*" Taggart roared.

Jack drew his cutlass as men rushed at him from the darkness. They formed a circle and Taggart pushed his way through them with a smile of triumph.

"I have you this time, Vincent," he said. He turned to one of his men. "Let's see what he's smuggling."

Honesty pulled away from his captors and ran to Jack's side. "I told 'em you was doin' it for a friend," he gasped.

Taggart laughed. "If you mean Rummy Culbert," he said, "I gave him the goods to snare you!"

The lid was prized off one of the kegs.

"This should put you away for a long stretch," chuckled Taggart, and reached inside for the tobacco. His expression changed. The little barrel contained nothing but sand! "Break open the others!" he roared.

The men set to with the butts of their muskets. There wasn't an ounce of tobacco in a single keg; nothing but sand.

Jack and Honesty were just as bewildered, but also very relieved. They smiled at Taggart, who ground his teeth and kicked the kegs in his frustration.

"Well, Mr Taggart," laughed Jack, "it seems that Rummy's snared both of us!"

However, Taggart was still determined to bring Jack to justice. The tobacco had to be somewhere, and he had no doubt that Rummy knew where it was. Somehow he had used Jack as a decoy, and while the Customs men were setting their ambush, the cunning old devil had hidden the tobacco somewhere else. He ordered his men to bind the prisoners, and then the whole party set off to Rummy's cottage.

When they arrived, Taggart pounded on the door with his fists. It was opened by Nan, who was draped in black from head to foot. She sobbed bitterly and tears rolled down her crumpled cheeks.

Taggart stared at her in some surprise. "Where's your husband?" he asked.

"Murderer! Murderer!" cried Nan, and tried to shut the door in his face.

"What the devil are you talking about?" said Taggart, sticking his foot in the door. "Where is he?"

"Dead! Dead!" wailed Nan, mopping her face with a kerchief. "And you killed him!"

"Dead?" gasped Taggart.

"He come back from you with his heart broken,"

sobbed Nan. "It was the shame of it all, and you forced him to do it."

Taggart pushed her to one side. This was some sort of trick. Rummy was probably climbing out of the bedroom window at that very moment. He strode across the poky little living room and flung open the door.

Rummy lay on top of a roughly-made coffin, wearing a nightshirt. His hands were crossed over his breast. On either side of the coffin a tall candle was burning. Parson Leatherby, a plump, pink-faced man knelt at Rummy's side. He turned as Taggart came into the bedroom and heaved himself to his feet.

"How dare you profane this solemn hour!" he brayed.

"Forgive me, Reverend," stammered Taggart. "But I thought – "

"Are you made of stone, man?" the fat parson continued. "Take off your hat!"

"I beg your pardon," Taggart apologised, whipping it off quickly.

Nan pushed her way into the room and flung herself on the body, howling loudly.

The Reverend Leatherby looked sadly at the stricken widow and then led Taggart back into the living room.

"Before he died, he told me everything," he said sadly.

"He didn't mention anything about tobacco, did he?" asked Taggart, who wasn't a man who gave up easily.

"I don't know how you're going to live with your guilt, Mr Taggart," the parson replied. "But if it's any consolation to you, his last words were 'I forgive him!'" Leatherby ushered Taggart – now somewhat shamefaced – to the door. "The funeral is at Farnmouth; St Peters by the Sea. I trust I shall see you there tomorrow. Good night, sir."

Taggart rejoined his men and the parson shut the door firmly.

"I suggest you cut us loose, Mr Taggart," said Jack coolly. "Your chief witness is no longer . . . available. And there's no law against importing sand."

Taggart nodded briefly, and the two prisoners were cut free.

"Don't look so smug, Vincent," Taggart warned. "I shall nail you one day, I promise you!" He looked back at the cottage. "It's galling to think that it's probably my money that'll pay for that old villain's funeral!"

The Customs men marched away, and to Honesty's surprise Jack knocked at the cottage door.

Nan peered out suspiciously. "What do you want?" she asked.

Jack pushed past her and went into the bedroom, followed by Honesty. Parson Leatherby opened his mouth to protest, and Jack shoved him firmly against the wall. Then he took out his snuffbox and sprinkled a pinch under Rummy's nostrils.

The corpse sneezed loudly and sat up.

"Praise the Lord!" intoned Honesty. "A miracle!"

Rummy sneezed again and climbed off the coffin.

"You old rogue!" chuckled Jack.

"This is all my doing, Mr Vincent," confessed the parson. "Rummy was forced to betray you. He came to me for advice, and I thought up this little charade."

Old Rummy hopped round the bedroom, chuckling gleefully and scratching himself. "Taggart can't touch you, Jack boy, 'cos there's no evidence against you. And he can't touch me, 'cos I'm dead."

"And where's the tobacco?" asked Jack.

Cackling with triumph, Rummy lifted the lid of the coffin; it was full of Negrohead tobacco.

"Tomorrow we shall transport it safely to Farnmouth, to the funeral," the parson explained. "Could you obtain a suitable cart, Mr Vincent?"

"Why me?" said Jack.

"You did agree to get it to Farnmouth," Rummy reminded him.

"Yes, but that was when I thought you were sick."

"Sick?" repeated Rummy. "Damnation, a few minutes ago I was dead as a doornail. You can't get no sicker than that!"

The following morning, Jack and Honesty drove up to Rummy's cottage with a horse and cart. They were met by Parson Leatherby who helped them load up the coffin.

"Mr Culbert and his wife have gone on ahead," he sniggered. "He thought it unwise to ride with his own coffin."

He climbed up beside them on the cart, and they set off towards Farnmouth.

"You've no objections to aiding and abetting smugglers?" Jack asked him.

"Since, like most of my fellows, I drink your brandy and tea," replied the parson with a smile, "why shouldn't I help you when you've needed me? Besides," he added, "Rummy has promised me a third of the proceeds from the sale of the tobacco. For the Steeple Fund, of course."

"Of course," smiled Jack.

"Rummy advised taking the cliff road," said the parson. "That way we can easily get rid of the evidence if we run into trouble."

"Did he expect any?" said Honesty quickly.

"No, no! I have no doubt our progress will be without incident or hinder," the parson replied.

Meanwhile, a strange scene was taking place in Taggart's office. Nan had come bursting in, screaming, "Sacrilege!"

"There'll be no funeral," she told Taggart. "That tobacco you was looking for has been put in my poor man's coffin by Jack Vincent!"

Taggart shot to his feet.

"He's smuggling it into Farnmouth," Nan cried. "And he's bamboozled the poor Reverend to ride with him."

Taggart hastily buckled on his sword-belt. "Which road are they taking to Farnmouth?" he demanded.

"Along the cliffs," Nan told him. "But you'll need every man you've got."

On the cliff road the coffin bumped and swayed on the cart, and Jack cracked his whip over his horse's ears. The parson clutched the seat, his large paunch wobbling from side to side. He gasped. "This is supposed to be a funeral, not a chariot race. I'm a poor traveller at the best of times."

Suddenly, Honesty caught sight of Taggart and his men galloping up the road behind them.

"It's Taggart!" he warned.

Jack glanced over his shoulder and urged his horse to greater efforts. The parson clasped his hands and began to pray earnestly. The cart tore along, rocking dangerously; its wheels were only inches from the edge of the cliff, but Taggart continued to gain on them.

"Looks like he'll have to be buried at sea!" gasped Jack, bringing the horse to a halt. "I'll hold them off. You tip the coffin over the cliff."

While the parson and Honesty heaved the coffin from the cart, Jack fired at the oncoming riders and they reared and wheeled in confusion. Only Taggart came on at the gallop, for he could see Honesty and the parson heaving the coffin towards the edge of the cliff. He dismounted and levelled his pistol at Jack.

"Put it down, man!" he shouted.

Honesty and the parson obeyed as Taggart's men rode up to join him.

"This time, I've got you for certain," Taggart said to Jack, as they bound him.

The men were reluctant to break open the coffin, until

Taggart shouted angrily at them: "It holds tobacco, you fools!"

As two of his men cautiously began prizing off the lid, Taggart turned to Jack. "How could you add to an old woman's grief?" he said with contempt. "If she hadn't told me where to find you – "

"Nan informed on us?" Jack cut in.

"Why would she do that?" said Honesty.

The lid was finally lifted from the coffin and Taggart looked eagerly inside. Then his jaw dropped open, as for a second time his hopes were dashed. In the coffin were several large bundles of old clothes; but not a single leaf of tobacco!

Several miles away, at the rear entrance of Mr Rook's store in Farnmouth, stood Rummy's handcart covered by a tarpaulin.

Nan, Rummy and Mr Rook came out into the little alley, all of them apparently well content.

"First class tobacco, Mr Culbert," said Rook.

"And a first class price," chuckled Nan, jingling a bag of money.

Rummy chuckled and took up his cart. "Sorry we can't do no more business with you," he said to Rook. "But we're moving on to pastures new."

"You could teach Jack Vincent a trick or two!" laughed Mr Rook.

"Oh, I don't know about that," smiled Rummy. "I think he knows most of 'em by now."

Nan helped him to steady the cart. "Rummy's giving up the smuggling business," she said. "It's bad for his health."

"I should just think it is!" Rummy cackled as they moved off down the alley. "This last little caper damn near had me in my coffin!"

On the cliffs, Taggart, who had searched the clothes thoroughly for any trace of tobacco, found a note at the bottom of the coffin.

"The Last Will and Testament of Rummy Culbert," he read aloud. "I leave these old clothes and unwanted chattels to the Fund for Distressed Mariners. And to my friends I leave the knowledge that thanks to them I am going on to a better and richer life."

"I bet he is, the crafty old devil!" laughed Jack Vincent.

CHAPTER SEVEN

RUMMY CULBERT had tricked all of them. Though Taggart did his best to keep it dark, the story was all over the borough in a matter of days. The Customs Officer lost face, and it made him more determined than ever to put Jack behind bars.

But the smuggler was too cunning for him. Jack landed his illicit cargoes in a hundred different places. Often he would 'sow the crop' off-shore, anchoring his barrels under water and marking the place with a buoy made from a piece of drift-wood. Then, when he beached the *Mary Jane*, the only thing Taggart's men would find was half a dozen empty lobster pots. It was a dangerous game, but Jack enjoyed it, and soon his secret storeroom deep under the Quayhaven cliffs was crammed with contraband.

Honesty spent most of his time at the cottage. He ran errands and took messages, he helped with the cooking – he was a good cook – and foraged along the shore for pieces of driftwood to burn on the fire. When Jack grew tired of his endless chatter, he would throw Honesty out. The boy soon learnt the warning signs and would stop prattling in time to avoid eviction.

Sometimes, storms prevented Jack making a 'run' and then he would march moodily along the cliffs, cursing the sea and praying for fine weather. It was on days like these that Jack thought back to his time in the Navy. He recognised that his impatience with authority had brought about his downfall. He had been ambitious, anxious to prove himself. England had been at war and surely, he reasoned, it was better to sink an enemy ship than to obey every piffling order. But the naval big-wigs had tried to put him in his place and quoted the traditions of the Service at him, until he could bear it no longer. He was a loner now and could do as he pleased but there were times when he regretted his impulsive resignation. The dangers of smuggling and the risks he ran every day gave him the excitement he needed – but he was still restless.

One afternoon when the wind tore at the roof and howled round the walls with maniac fury, Jack sat glumly by the window while Honesty idled away the time reading the tea-leaves at the bottom of his mug. He didn't like what he saw.

"It looks bad, Mister Jack," he muttered.

"Yes," Jack replied, watching the scurrying clouds with a practised eye, "and its going to get worse."

"There's a tall dark stranger, I reckon," Honesty continued mysteriously.

Jack turned from the window, surprised to find Honesty crouched over an empty mug.

"Mmmm . . . I see a lady . . . and what's this? Marriage?"

Marriage was the last thing on Jack's mind. He went over to the table and peered into the mug. Honesty looked up at him.

"Can you see anything?"

Jack nodded. "Tea-leaves."

"Don't mock me, Mister Jack," said Honesty. "It's an art, my Aunty Olwen says. She taught me, you see. The tea-leaves never lie."

"That's bilge-water," replied Jack, who had no time for superstition.

Honesty looked into the mug once more and drew in his breath sharply.

"Now what?" sighed Jack.

Honesty looked up at him nervously. "It's nothing," he

lied. "You're – you're going to be famous as Nelson, you are."

"I doubt it!"

"No," Honesty persisted, "it's true! I see great deeds of honour and glory. And they'll award you hundreds of medals – maybe even a knighthood. They'll raise marble statues of you – tall as a mast!"

He gestured dramatically, indicating the magnificence of the statues and something fell out of his pocket. He picked it up quickly, but Jack had seen it.

"What have you got there?" he asked quickly.

Honesty backed away. "Something I found," he stammered. "It's nothing – nothing important."

Jack held out his hand. "Let me see!"

"No – I – "

"*Hand it over!*"

Honesty reached the door.

"You stole it, didn't you?" Jack accused.

"I found it, Mister Jack!" protested Honesty. "It's mine!"

"You're a liar!"

"Not always!"

Jack held out his hand. "Give it to me, boy!" he ordered.

Honesty shook his head.

"Very well, then," said Jack calmly. "You can get out. I've had enough of you."

"But if the wind drops?" asked Honesty. "What about the run?"

Jack's answer to this was to grab Honesty by the scruff of the neck and throw him out of the cottage.

Honesty, who was used to it by now, picked himself up, ran to a safe distance, and then shouted back: "I'll tell you what I really saw! You with a bullet in your head, and that woman with you!"

"What woman?"

"The one I saw in the tea-leaves," Honesty yelled. "And that's why you won't take me, isn't it? Oh, I know! You want to see your fancy foreign lady and be alone with her!" And he began swearing at Jack in Welsh.

A hand clasped his shoulder and spun him round.

A tall, wild-looking man with an eye-patch and a long ragged scar down his face, glared down at him. It was the tall, dark stranger! thought Honesty. He broke from the man's grasp and darted off up the cliff path.

Jack smiled at the stranger as he approached.

"How are you, Jack?" said the man with a crooked smile.

"Good to see you, Mr Roach!" said Jack. "It's been a long time. Who gave you that scar?"

"I ran up against a bit of trouble, Jack," Roach answered. "It laid me up for a while . . ."

"Who was it?" Jack persisted.

But Roach merely shook his head. "Some friends of mine," he said.

Jack nodded. In the smuggling game it was wise not to ask too many questions. If Roach didn't want to tell him, that was his business.

"It's a long time since we traded, Mr Roach. Or is this merely a friendly visit?"

Roach rubbed his bony nose and pulled his ragged coat closer around him. "I'm getting myself back together, bit by bit." He put his head on one side like a questioning dog. "Thought you might give me a helping hand. I've got a buyer, ye see. He wants some brandy and claret – only the best claret – the proper Bordeaux stuff."

"How much?"

"Two casks and six tubs of brandy," Roach told him. "Thing is, Jack, I'm a bit short at the moment, and I

87

was wondering if you'd take payment on delivery, so to speak?"

Jack considered this for a moment, and finally nodded. "When d'you want it?"

"Two days time?" Roach suggested. "I don't suppose you need anyone for tub carrying?"

Jack was surprised. Roach had been one of the leading smugglers on the coast. Yet here he was asking for the lowly job of tub-carrier.

"Every little helps," shrugged Roach. "Things being as bad as they are. How about a guinea for the night?"

This was the standard fee, but Jack shook his head. He worked alone and he told Roach so.

Roach nodded. "I understand, Jack boy," he said quietly. He held out his hand. "All fair and square?"

They shook hands once, and the bargain was made.

"Would you care for a drink?" asked Jack.

"When I get the goods," said Roach grimly. "Then we'll have a drink, eh?" He pointed to his remaining eye. "One thing's certain; I still got a good eye for a bargain, eh?"

The following morning, Honesty went to see Sarah at Westmore Hall. He took with him the mysterious object that he had refused to show Jack. It was a miniature in an oval frame; a portrait of a girl with long dark hair. He had found it in a drawer in Jack's bedroom and he was sure that the girl was the smuggler's sweetheart; and equally certain she was French. Jack often went to St Malo, and on those trips he went alone. Honesty, who was fond of Sarah, decided with some indignation that she ought to know all about it.

"I saw it all in the tea-leaves, Miss Sarah," said Honesty as they walked together in the garden. "She's his sweetheart."

Sarah was used to Honesty's stories and paid him very little attention.

"That's why he kicked me out," he persisted. "All because of her."

"Sweetheart indeed!" laughed Sarah. "I expect he caught you stealing, didn't he?"

Honesty shook his head. "It wasn't like that, Miss Sarah. It was something I found, see?"

He gave her the miniature.

"It fell out of his pocket," he lied glibly. "Carries it with him all the time. I was going to give it back when he threw me out. She's French, I reckon."

Sarah could see that the girl was beautiful. She felt a twinge of jealousy.

"I've seen him on the boat, gazing at it," Honesty went on, adding to his story with considerable imagination. "He thought I was asleep. It all fits, you see? Just like in the tea-leaves."

"I don't believe a word of it!" said Sarah, a bit too vehemently. "I expect it's – it's one of his family – a sister – or – or – a cousin perhaps."

"The leaves never lie," said Honesty darkly. "That's Mister Jack's fancy woman. I know it is."

And so it was when Jack sailed the *Mary Jane* through the narrow channel that night, and out into the open sea, there was a stowaway hidden under a tarpaulin.

Honesty grinned as he watched the lugger move away from the shore. Mister Jack was in for a shock.

But other eyes were on the little boat also. On a clifftop, Tarrant stood with Roach and patted him on the back. Roach had become a Customs man and had kept this knowledge from the smugglers he now helped to trap.

"Well, thanks to you, Mr Roach," he whispered, "Vincent's smuggling days are nearly over."

It was a calm night with a waning moon often obscured behind the clouds. Jack searched the horizon but there was no sign of the Revenue cutter. He eased the tiller round a couple of points and took a swig from a bottle of wine. Then his eyes narrowed as the tarpaulin, forward, began to move. Finally Sarah emerged from under it.

"What the devil are you doing on my boat?" gasped Jack, hardly able to believe his senses.

"I stowed away," said Sarah sweetly. "To keep you company."

"Why?" said Jack. "What in hell's name is this about?"

"You know well enough," Sarah replied tartly.

"Don't tack!"

"The girl," Sarah explained.

Jack looked puzzled. "What girl?" he said.

"Your French piece," Sarah tossed the miniature to him contemptuously.

"So that's it," muttered Jack, putting it quickly into his pocket.

"Well?"

"Well what?"

"Is it true?"

"What do you think?"

"I – I don't *know!*" cried Sarah angrily.

"By God, I'll strangle that boy!" muttered Jack.

"Who is she?" persisted Sarah.

"A friend," Jack answered.

"A friend? Whose picture you carry everywhere?"

"Is that what the little liar told you?" said Jack.

"I thought I meant something to you," snapped Sarah.

Jack's eyes blazed with anger. "And I to you!" he said bitterly.

"Take me ashore!" demanded Sarah.

"The hell I will," Jack replied. "You wanted to come, you wanted to keep me company. Then you shall!"

Sarah began to think that perhaps she had made a fool of herself after all.

"I'm sorry," she said. "I didn't mean it. Take me back."

"It's too late," said Jack shortly. "Come here!"

Sarah stepped unsteadily to the stern and sat down ungracefully as the little boat bobbed over a wave.

"Take the helm!" Jack ordered.

"But I can't – "

"Take it!"

Sarah grabbed the tiller and looked nervously up at Jack standing beside her.

"Can you feel the wind on your left cheek?" he said sharply.

Sarah nodded.

"Well keep it there. If the sail starts to flap, ease her off to port. That's left," Jack added sarcastically.

"I know!" replied Sarah.

"Good," smiled Jack. "Now you're here, you can work your passage."

The sail began flapping.

"You're going off course!" he shouted angrily. "Bring her round."

He put a hand to the tiller and brought the boat on course again. "Now keep her there," he said to Sarah. The sail filled and the *Mary Jane* seemed to dance forward. Jack snuggled down among the nets at the bottom of the boat. "Wake me in a couple of hours," he said.

"But I can't sail a boat!" said Sarah in a sudden panic.

"Not yet," Jack replied with a grin. "But you're learning."

It was now a question of pride for Sarah. She stared grimly ahead with her hands tight on the tiller. Although she was frightened out of her wits, she was determined not to show it. Jack, who was only pretending to be asleep, watched her from the bottom of the boat and smiled to himself. By the time he'd finished with her, she would wish she'd stayed at home.

They reached the French coast at dawn, and after

beaching the *Mary Jane*, Jack and Sarah set off through the woods which led to the little fishing port of St Malo. The tall smuggler strode along purposefully, and it was all Sarah could do to keep up with him. He never looked round at her, and remained silent. In fact, he seemed to be ignoring her completely. After a while, Sarah could bear it no longer.

"Where are we going?" she said timidly.

"To find you lodgings," Jack replied without looking round.

"Can't I come with you?"

"No. I've a cargo to arrange."

"Where?" asked Sarah.

"That's my business."

Sarah was indignant. "Is that all you can say?" Jack sighed. "The place is too damned rough for – someone like you," he explained.

"Can't you do better than that?" said Sarah, beginning to simmer.

Jack marched on in silence.

"I'm not going to a lodging house," said Sarah resentfully.

Jack stopped. "Very well," he said irritably. "But don't say I didn't warn you!"

The inn Jack led her to was called La Carmagnole – a well known haunt of both French and English smugglers. Inside, a dozen or so seafaring men sat drinking and playing cards. They took no notice of the two strangers. Stretched out in front of the fire, and snoring loudly, lay a huge fat man with a curly black beard. In one corner, a tough-looking seaman was talking earnestly to a tall young woman. When she saw Jack, she ran to greet him, and Sarah stared at her with astonishment. It was the girl in the miniature!

"Oh Jack," she said, embracing him warmly. "It's been

so long since you were last here. It is good to see you again!"

The seaman glowered jealously at them. And so did Sarah. Jack turned to her. "This is Sarah," he said. And then to Sarah, "This is Jeanette."

Jeanette and Sarah looked each other up and down and neither liked what they saw. They smiled and nodded at each other coldly.

"Your wife?" Sarah asked Jack.

Jack shook his head.

"You're welcome," smiled Jeanette falsely. She took Jack's arm and led him to an empty table. Sarah followed.

"Would you like a comb, my dear?" said Jeanette maliciously, looking at Sarah's tangled and windswept hair.

"No thank you," Sarah replied coldly, and sat opposite them with as much dignity as she could muster.

Jeanette turned her attention to Jack. "She is charming, is she not? And so very young." She smiled at Sarah, but her eyes were cold. A serving girl brought them wine and Jeanette poured two glasses, completely ignoring Sarah. She gazed into Jack's eyes. "What are you here for?" she asked softly.

Sarah took the bottle and poured some for herself.

"Bordeaux claret," Jack replied to Jeanette. "The best vintage."

She touched his arm. "I have just what you require," she said softly.

Sarah watched every move and every expression. It seemed clear to her that Honesty had been right from the beginning. In her eyes, Jeanette was a scheming hussy, intent on twisting Jack round her little finger. She wished with all her heart that she'd stayed in England and blamed her own foolishness for letting Honesty talk her into stowing away aboard the *Mary Jane*. But she was determined not to let the French girl get the better of her so she kept her temper and remained silent. When Jeanette took Jack by the hand and led him down into the cellars, Sarah smiled politely and followed, as if she had also been invited.

The cellars of La Carmagnole were filled to the roof with great vats of wine. There were tuns and hogsheads. There were smaller barrels too: casks, ankers and half-ankers.

A cask was broached and Jack tasted it carefully. It was a fine wine, and he nodded his approval.

Jeanette leant back against the barrel, smiling at him seductively. "Shall we say fifteen English guineas?" she smiled.

"Ten," said Jack flatly.

The girl shook her head. "It is the best. The very best," she replied. "But I will take twelve, because it is you, my dear Jack!"

"If your man loads it," said Jack with a grin.

"Where is your boat?"

"Point de la Roche," Jack told her, taking a leather pouch from his pocket and counting twelve guineas into her hand. "Six tubs of brandy and two casks of claret."

Jeanette kissed him on the cheek to seal the bargain. Sarah pointedly ignored her.

"I'll see that it is loaded immediately," whispered Jeanette.

Jack's merchandise was carefully loaded on to a farm-cart by the big seaman who had been talking to Jeanette earlier. His name was Marcel, and he was very much in love with her, and very suspicious of Jack.

"Who is this Englishman?" he asked Jeanette angrily.

"Only a friend," she replied, secretly pleased that her lover was jealous. "I trade with him, nothing more. And

94

the sooner you get the barrels on board his boat, the sooner he will leave."

"Then I shall take them immediately," Marcel replied.

By evening, Jack's cargo was safely hidden on board the *Mary Jane*, and in La Carmagnole, Jeanette and he, together with Sarah and an extremely disgruntled Marcel, sat down to supper. Sarah smouldered with resentment and Marcel glared at Jack while Jeanette deliberately went on flirting with him. Sarah noticed how angry the Frenchman was becoming and so, after downing another glass of wine, she across the table and said to Jack: "She's your fancy woman, isn't she?"

Jeanette laughed.

"Don't laugh at me, you trollop!" cried Sarah.

Jeanette's eyes narrowed. "Be careful, mademoiselle."

Sarah poured herself another large glass of wine.

"You've had enough," said Jack.

"More than enough," snapped Sarah. "Do you think I'm blind?"

"No," mocked Jeanette. "Just stupid!"

Sarah rose unsteadily. The inn seemed to spin before her eyes. "Stupid, yes," she said loudly. "Very stupid. I've been very stupid, haven't I?"

"There's no need to tell everyone," said Jack, trying to make her sit down.

"Why shouldn't I tell them?" Sarah shouted. "Why shouldn't I tell them she's your fancy woman?"

"Taisez-vous!" hissed Jeanette.

Sarah leant forward and snapped her fingers in the girl's face.

"You see them?" she said to Marcel. "Look at them! You know, don't you? You must know!"

"Know?" said Marcel, who didn't understand English.

Sarah switched to French. "You must know that they

95

are lovers," she said rapidly. "They're deceiving both of us."

"Then it is true!" roared Marcel, getting to his feet. "You lied to me!" he said to Jeanette, and trembling with fury, he drew his sword. Jeanette screamed and tried to hide behind Jack.

"Coward!" shouted Sarah, completely carried away. "Coward!"

"English pig!" snarled Marcel, waving his sword threateningly.

"Don't be a fool!" said Jack, trying to calm him down.

"He says you're a fool," explained Sarah to Marcel in French.

"It is true!" sobbed Marcel. "I am a fool. And a cuckold!"

"I won't fight you," Jack told him. "There's nothing to fight about."

"Are you frightened you might lose?" jeered Sarah.

"Will you shut up!" shouted Jack, beginning to lose his temper.

With a roar, Marcel charged at him like an enraged bull, and would have cut him in half if Jack hadn't defended himself with a chair.

Jack knew that Marcel couldn't be reasoned with, so he drew his cutlass and prepared to defend himself.

"This is your doing!" Jeanette screamed at Sarah.

"You deserve everything you get!" Sarah yelled back.

Jeanette grabbed her by the hair, and they struggled together, all caution thrown to the winds. Jeanette overbalanced and fell, with Sarah on top of her. Marcel charged at Jack, swinging wildly. Jack, who didn't want to harm him, defended himself coolly, but Marcel kept up the attack with undiminished fury. He would cut the Englishman into little pieces, and feed them to the fishes. But the wildness of his blows proved his undoing. He swung at Jack viciously, missed him completely, lost his balance and crashed to the floor.

"You wait till I get you home!" snarled Jack as he pulled Sarah off Jeanette and bustled her out of the door.

"I'm not coming with you!" she sobbed, but a fusillade of pistol shots made her change her mind, and the two of them fled up the village street with Marcel and his friends behind them.

They reached the safety of the trees and looked back. The Frenchmen were still coming. A bullet whined over their heads and ricocheted off one of the trees. Jack grabbed Sarah and pulled her forward.

They stumbled on through the darkness until at last they could see the moon shining on the waters of the bay. By now their pursuers were close behind them.

"Get to the boat!" Jack commanded.

Sarah hesitated.

"Damn you, girl! Do as I say!" roared Jack, drawing his cutlass and turning to face Marcel and his friends.

Sarah ran over the sand-dunes to where the *Mary Jane* lay at anchor. Jack had counted the shots: There had been three: and three men were running towards him. They had had no time to reload their pistols, and he'd taken on greater odds than this.

As Marcel rushed him, Jack side-stepped and hit him neatly on the point of his chin. The Frenchman went down as if poleaxed. The other two cut at him inexpertly and Jack gave a tremendous yell of fury – deliberately designed to unnerve them – and counter-attacked. He cut the first man across the cheek, and then swung round and sliced open the other's knee. They howled with pain and dropped their weapons.

Jack ran to the boat and pushed off. He picked up Sarah and tossed her aboard as if she was a sack of potatoes. Heaving himself over the gunwhale, he hoisted the sail and set course for home. He did all this in silence, never even looking at Sarah, who sat trembling in the stern. The race through the woods had sobered her, and now she was beginning to feel very ashamed of herself. Nevertheless, she summoned what little dignity she could and stared straight ahead, determined that Jack would be the first to speak.

"You and your damn jealousy!" he burst out as the coast of France receded. "There's nothing to be jealous about!"

"Nothing?" said Sarah.

"Nothing!" repeated Jack angrily. "And what's more, you damn near got me shot!"

Sarah sniffed. "Pity they missed," she muttered.

"Thank you," he said, pulling in the mainsail. "Did you enjoy the voyage, Miss Morton?"

"I'll never forget it!" Sarah replied solemnly.

Jack smiled grimly. "It's not over yet," he said. "And because of you we've left France too early. It'll still be light when we reach England."

By dawn a stiff wind from the south-west was causing the *Mary Jane* to buck and dip over the waves. Tired though he was, Jack never relaxed his vigilance. The Channel was a dangerous place and an error of judgement could cost them their lives. Still, he was making good time, the cargo was safe, and if his luck held he would avoid the coastal patrols.

Some time during the afternoon, Sarah was scanning the horizon when she caught sight of a Revenue cutter. Jack recognised its rig immediately.

These fast little ships watched out for smugglers and were able to board any craft the Customs men thought to be suspicious.

Jack steered the *Mary Jane* as close to the wind as he dared, hoping to outrun the larger vessel. Both jib and

mainsail were as close-hauled as possible. A cannon-ball sent a plume of water skywards, only yards away from the lugger, and a second later they heard the hollow boom of the cutter's cannon.

The Customs men tried vainly to sail as close to the wind as Jack in an attempt to overhaul him, but instead they were forced to come about and sailed past the lugger's stern. There was a ragged volley of musket fire, and Jack spun round, let go of the tiller, and collapsed on top of his cargo. The boat swung wildly, but Sarah kept her head and grabbed the tiller. More by luck than judgement, she managed to put her back on course.

She called to Jack and a faint movement told her that he was still alive; she looked round at the Revenue cutter, determined to outrun her. All she could do was to sail on the course already set.

The coast of England was a welcome sight. Sarah could see a narrow channel ahead. Gritting her teeth, she kept on course and sailed through without damage. The Revenue cutter, unable to follow her, veered off into deeper water, and cheated of success, turned out to sea in search of easier prey.

It was only when the *Mary Jane* grounded gently on the beach that Sarah finally let go the tiller and crouched down to cradle Jack's head in her arms. There was a trickle of blood from his forehead where a musket ball had grazed his temple. He stirred, his eyes opened, and he looked up at Sarah. Then he felt his head. He struggled to his feet and swayed, blinking away the dizziness and looking round in astonishment at the cliffs and the rocky beach.

He turned to Sarah. "You outran the cutter?" he said incredulously.

Sarah nodded wearily.

"Then you must have come through the Gut!"

"I must have done," said Sarah proudly.

"You could've ripped her bottom out!" roared Jack.

Sarah flushed angrily. "Is that all the thanks I get?"

Jack was just going to take her in his arms, when he saw the small figure of Honesty Evans running towards them.

"Quick, Mister Jack!" shouted Honesty. "There's Customs men all over the place!"

But his warning was too late, and as they climbed out of the *Mary Jane*, they were surrounded by a group of Excise men, and Taggart walked slowly towards them with the one-eyed Roach by his side.

"Well, Vincent," Taggart smiled. "You've led us a dance, ain't you?"

Jack looked curiously at Roach. "You, a shark?" he asked.

"Excise man," corrected Roach with a wicked chuckle. "And what have we here? A young lady of standing? I'm surprised at you, Miss Morton!"

"She's no part of it – " said Jack.

"You tell that to the magistrate," Roach replied.

"To think you were a smuggler once," said Jack bitterly to Roach.

"Aye, I was once," Roach replied. "Now I've turned against 'em." He pointed to the patch on his eye. "The Durston gang made me change my course. But I've put paid to them. Jailed the lot, didn't I, Mr Taggart? And a few others since. Doing well, I am."

"It's likely you'll get promoted for helping to put Jack Vincent away," said Taggart triumphantly.

Sarah stepped forward. "Putting him away for what?" she asked.

"You know well enough, Miss Morton," Taggart answered.

"No I do not, sir."

"For running contraband," said Taggart.

"Mr Vincent took me sailing," Sarah told him. "He was teaching me to handle a boat."

Taggart sighed. It was the tallest story he had ever heard. "Search it, Mr Roach," he ordered.

Roach climbed into the *Mary Jane* and began to rummage. After a moment or two he looked up, frowning. "There's nothin' here!" he gasped.

"Of course there isn't," said Sarah coolly.

It was Taggart's turn to leap into the boat. He saw immediately that, apart from some nets and a few lobster pots, the *Mary Jane* was empty.

Jack looked at Sarah, and somehow managed to keep a straight face. "It seems your promotion will have to wait, Roach," he murmured. "And now, if you'll excuse us, gentlemen, I must escort Miss Morton home."

As they walked away from the thwarted Excise men, Jack could hardly wait to find out what had happened to his cargo. When they were safely out of earshot, Sarah whispered: "I threw the barrels overboard."

Jack looked at her. "You stow away on my boat – get me into a fight in France – I'm wounded by the sharks – and end up with nothing!"

"Except your life!" replied Sarah indignantly.

Jack roared with laughter. "When do we sail again?" he asked her with a mocking look in his eye.

"Never!" said Sarah.

CHAPTER EIGHT

It took Jack several weeks to forgive Honesty for the trouble and mischief he'd caused. As punishment he made the wretched boy slave for him until he was almost dropping with fatigue. But Honesty never complained. He merely squared his meagre shoulders and took his punishment manfully, knowing it was deserved. And secretly Jack admired him for it. The boy had a quality known in those days as 'bottom'. This meant spirit or courage, and his was shortly to be tested to the utmost.

Barely a week after he had finally made his peace with "Mister Jack", Honesty was walking to Westmore Hall for a navigation lesson with Captain Konig when he was seen by a press gang.

Because of the harshness of life in the navy of those days, very few men volunteered, so the law allowed parties of sailors to scour the coastal areas and capture whoever they could. They were called press gangs because they pressed, or forced, men to join up against their will.

Immediately, the lieutenant in charge caught sight of Honesty he barked out an order, and the gang broke into a run, fanning out behind the boy as they came after him. Try as he might, he simply could not throw them off, and his luck ran out when he lost his balance as he ran downhill and went head over heels to the bottom. The pressgang, led by their officer, ran down to the prostrate boy panting hard and sweating.

Lieutenant Scott-Ponsonby was an ambitious young man, tall and with an athlete's build. He considered himself to be wasted as a Press Master, and chafed under the restraint. At the same time, he was determined that he would be noted for his efficiency and the zeal with which he carried out his duties. He looked down at the ragged lad with a feeling of satisfaction. The boy was obviously sound in wind and limb.

"Get up!" ordered Ponsonby.

Honesty struggled to his feet, panting hard.

"How old are you?" Ponsonby asked.

"Fifteen, I think – " began Honesty.

"You think!" cut in Ponsonby quickly. "You're eighteen if you're a day!"

Honesty looked shocked. "Oh no I'm not, mister, I know I – "

Again, Ponsonby interrupted him. "If I say you're eighteen – then you're eighteen. Bind him!"

Honesty was quickly pinioned and his hands tied behind him.

"You're very lucky," chuckled the Lieutenant, "I'm giving you the chance to defend England against tyranny!"

"But I'm Welsh," said Honesty helplessly.

"Don't quibble!" replied Ponsonby coldly.

The press gang marched away with their latest victim, unaware that the capture had been seen by Jack Vincent. There was nothing he could do. Pressing men for the navy was quite legal, and he watched the sailors taking Honesty away with a heavy heart.

Meanwhile, at Westmore Hall, Captain Konig was still waiting for his pupil.

"I don't understand the boy," he said to Sarah. "We were doing so well, so very well. He seemed truly interested – "

"Don't be too disappointed, Grandfather," Sarah replied. "Honesty's restless – he wants excitement."

Captain Konig looked at her ruefully. "He wants to be with Jack Vincent, you mean!"

Sarah smiled. "You forget that you'd been halfway round the world at his age," she said.

The old man nodded. "Very true," he admitted. "And I'd never opened a book. My schooling was the deck of a ship, my dear. I had a wonderful childhood, Sarah. I shall never forget the islands of the East Indies; their colours and sounds; the green-black forests . . ." He took his grand-daughter's hand and his eyes twinkled. "Now that was an education, Sarah!"

A moment later, Jack strode into the room, his face like a thundercloud. "Honesty won't be coming for his navigation lesson, Captain Konig," he said curtly.

Sarah looked at Jack with alarm, sensing something was wrong. "What's happened?" she said.

Jack shrugged. "A press gang's got him."

"But he's too young!" gasped Sarah.

"Is he?" Jack retorted. "I was put on a ship's books while I was still in the nursery."

"Then why are you angry?" asked Sarah.

Jack turned away from them, trying hard to conceal his true feelings. "Who says I am?" he parried. "The boy was useful to me, nothing more."

"Come now, Jack," said Sarah softly, "that isn't true. You know you cared for him."

Jack stared into the fire remembering how Honesty had saved his life; the rows they had had, and the good times too. He knew that the navy would have to break the boy's spirit. He'd seen it done to others . . .

"I shall seek a writ for Habeas Corpus," said Captain Konig.

"On what grounds, Captain?" asked Jack.

"On the grounds that the whole principle of impressment is an invasion of personal liberty," replied the captain.

Jack laughed bitterly. "You'll get short shrift from the

Admiralty," he retorted. "Pressing's been complained about since England had a navy."

"Then why does it continue?" said the captain.

"Because 'men-of-war must be manned'," quoted Jack.

"It's far worse than kidnap," said Captain Konig. "How can it be justified?"

" 'The safety of the state'," Jack replied ironically.

"Ah yes," nodded Konig. "Such a useful phrase!"

"Stop talking politics!" Sarah broke in angrily. "What about Honesty?"

"There's nothing we can do!" Jack told her.

The press gang's headquarters – the 'rondy' or rendez-vous – had been set up at The Raven. A Union Jack hung from an improvised flagpole over the door, and lurid recruiting posters in bold black type proclaimed the joys and rewards of life in the navy. They were couched in extravagant language, and even suggested that potential sailors would have the chance to go on voyages in search of buried treasure. It was all untrue, of course, but it helped to encourage the slow-witted.

Honesty was dragged through a crowd of curious village girls who were giggling at the sailors on guard, and taken into the tap-room where three or four fishermen, wearing chains, stood sullenly in a row guarded by a stolid cox-swain.

Ponsonby looked disdainfully at them.

"Who are these, Higgins?" he barked.

The coxswain drew himself up and saluted. "The magis-trate sent 'em, sir," he said.

Ponsonby shook his head. "I'll have no criminals."

"Smugglers, sir," explained the coxswain. "Good sea-men, all of 'em."

This was a very different kettle of fish and Ponsonby knew it. Some of the finest seamen in the navy had once been smugglers.

"Very well," he replied. "Put the rogues in the lock-up." He indicated Honesty. "And this one with 'em."

But Honesty ducked under the coxswain's arm and darted out of the inn before the astonished sailors had time to recover. As he ran out, he kicked a bench across the doorway and Lieutenant Ponsonby went sprawling in the dirt. By the time the coxswain had helped him to his feet and they had pushed their way through the crowd, Honesty was speeding up the road.

With his lungs almost bursting, he finally reached Westmore Hall and hammered on the door desperately. Jack had returned to his cottage, leaving Sarah and her grandfather wondering if there was anything they could do to secure Honesty's release.

"Don't let 'em take me, Miss Sarah," sobbed Honesty as she opened the door.

The exhausted boy followed her to Captain Konig's study.

"They say I'm eighteen, Captain Konig," he gasped as his two friends helped him to a chair. "Eighteen! How could they know? I don't even know myself! But I'm not, am I? Not eighteen! And anyhow – why should I have to go into the navy? Why should I, eh? I haven't done nothing wrong. Well – not lately I haven't."

"Did the press gang see you coming here?" asked the captain anxiously.

"I dunno. I don't think so," replied Honesty wearily. "They took me to The Raven. The rondy they call it. Holding fifteen men, they said." The boy looked up at them desperately. "Let me stay here, Captain Konig. I can easy get to Mister Jack's after dark. They'll never catch me then."

There was the sound of thunderous knocking at the main door. The press gang had arrived. Captain Konig pulled Honesty from the chair and bundled him into an adjoining room.

Sarah took a deep breath, smoothed down her dress, and walked slowly to the hall. She opened the door.

Lieutenant Ponsonby swept off his hat and bowed politely.

"We're after a deserter, ma'am," he said stiffly. "He was seen running to this house."

"A deserter?" repeated Sarah.

Ponsonby twitched with impatience. "I'm a Press Master, ma'am," he explained. "May I enter?"

Sarah flushed angrily. "No, sir, you may not," she said firmly. "You are exceeding your authority."

"I doubt it," sneered the young lieutenant. "It's signed by the Lords Commissioners of Admiralty. Do you question *their* authority?"

There was nothing Sarah could do but let him enter. Ponsonby sent two of the press gang round to the back of the house, and the rest of them followed him into Westmore Hall.

"Is this your house, ma'am?" he asked Sarah with studied politeness.

"My grandfather's," she replied.

"Then I wish to see him."

The lieutenant's supercilious manner finally stung Sarah to anger. "This is disgraceful!" she cried.

"I apologise," said Ponsonby arrogantly.

"Will you please leave!"

"When I have spoken to your grandfather."

In the study, Captain Konig eyed the young officer calmly.

Ponsonby bowed. "My name's Scott-Ponsonby, sir."

"Walter Konig," replied the Captain.

"I have reason to believe a young deserter is hiding

somewhere within this house, and so I ask your permission to search it."

"A deserter, eh?" said Captain Konig. "From which ship?"

Ponsonby hesitated. He knew that the captain's question was a tricky one to answer. He must proceed cautiously.

"From no ship, sir," he admitted reluctantly. "He was pressed – and escaped."

Captain Konig smiled, but his eyes were cold. "But surely, lieutenant," he said softly, "a man would have to be on a ship's books to be called a deserter."

"That is hardly relevant – " blustered the lieutenant.

"I'm afraid it is," persisted Konig. "And I believe you know it. So now would you kindly leave my house. There is no deserter here."

Some instinct told Ponsonby that the boy was in the house, despite Captain Konig's words. The old man was shielding him and had turned the word 'deserter' to his advantage.

"If you are sheltering the . . . person, I seek," said Ponsonby carefully, "you would do well to admit that he is here. If you lie to me, sir, and I find him, you will face prosecution." He paused and looked hard at Konig. "Where is he?"

The door burst open and Honesty stood, white-faced and trembling. "They didn't know I was here," he told the lieutenant. "I got in the back way, see?"

In silence, he held out his hands to be manacled, and without further ado the lieutenant and the press gang left Westmore Hall. Captain Konig turned to Sarah with tears in his eyes. "He could not bear to let me lie," he said softly. "Even to save him!"

Jack heard the news when Sarah rode over to the cottage later that afternoon. Ponsonby's pursuit of the boy was unreasonable, even vicious; and Jack was angry.

"He's young, you say?" he asked Sarah.

"Young, callous, and I'd think ambitious," she answered.

Jack tapped on the table with his forefinger, thinking hard. Scott-Ponsonby was a familiar name to him. He looked up at Sarah. "There's a Rear-Admiral Scott-Ponsonby," he muttered. "He could be a relative of this beggar. He's another arrogant swine. It obviously runs in the family!"

He unlocked his sea-chest, took out his lieutenant's jacket and shook the dust from it. Sarah stared up at him in amazement.

"You're going to invite Lieutenant Scott-Ponsonby for luncheon," Jack said softly.

After he had explained his plan, Sarah chuckled with glee and when she returned home, sat down immediately to write a flowery note inviting the young lieutenant to dine at Westmore Hall the following day.

The next day, punctually at noon, the lieutenant presented himself at Westmore Hall in answer to Sarah's invitation. He was slightly puzzled by it. She had seemed so resentful the previous day. Ponsonby put down her change of attitude to his good looks. He was a very conceited young man.

Captain Konig also welcomed him warmly and apologised for the unpleasantness of the previous day.

The meal was a splendid one, and Ponsonby drank rather more than was good for him, which was just as they had planned. Sarah plied him with more.

"Thank you, ma'am," said Lieutenant Ponsonby.

Sarah flapped her long lashes at him. "There's no need to be so formal, is there? You must call me Sarah, and we shall call you – ?"

Ponsonby reddened. "Percival," he said with an embarrassed smile.

"Percival," repeated Sarah, savouring the name langorously.

"Forgive me," interrupted Captain Konig, "but are you by chance related to Rear-Admiral Scott-Ponsonby?"

"My uncle, sir," smirked the lieutenant.

"I knew him well at one time," Captain Konig continued. "I would be so grateful if you would give him my regards when next you see him."

"Oh, I will, sir," Ponsonby assured him.

"He was something of a martinet, I remember," said Captain Konig.

"Oh, he still is," said Ponsonby. "And he's inclined to expect a great deal of me," he added with a nervous chuckle.

It seemed that the young man was rather scared of his illustrious uncle: a fact that Sarah and her grandfather were quick to notice.

"And do you take him as a model?" said the Captain.

"I believe in strong discipline – "

"Quite so."

Sarah leant towards him, her eyes soft and inviting. "How many men have you – er – recruited, Percival?" she purred.

"Seventeen, ma'am – " replied Ponsonby proudly.

"You must call me Sarah," she whispered.

"Er – Sarah," Ponsonby stammered. "Eleven seamen and six landsmen. They go to the receiving ship at Farnmouth at the end of the week."

"You've done well," said Captain Konig.

"I trust the Regulating Captain will think so," replied the lieutenant. "We must have men."

Sarah looked at him with admiration. "Indeed, we must," she murmured.

After luncheon, Sarah took Lieutenant Ponsonby into the sitting room, and explained that her grandfather always

111

had a little nap in the afternoon. "So I shall have you all to myself, shan't I?" she said, drawing him down beside her on the chaise-longue.

Ponsonby fingered his collar. It suddenly seemed to be rather tight. "Er – I don't wish to seem churlish, Miss Morton," he said, "but I think that I should shortly return to – "

"What nonsense, Percival," interrupted Sarah, putting her hand gently on his arm. "It's barely two."

Lieutenant Ponsonby inched away from her. The young woman was clearly infatuated with him. Such an entanglement so early in his career could harm his prospects of promotion. But the wretched girl refused to take the hint. Again she sidled up to him, and wedged him firmly against the arm of the chaise.

"I have so much to ask you," she murmured. "You lead such an adventurous life. Full of danger and excitement. Whilst I . . . You cannot imagine how dull my life is. And how seldom I meet anyone . . . *interesting*."

Ponsonby attempted to rise. "Oh, I would not say that I – "

Sarah pulled him down. "And I was so short with you yesterday," she continued, her soft lips only a few inches from his face. "And you were so – so stern, and so very *demanding*." She gave him what could only be described as a 'lingering look'. "Are you demanding, Percival?" she whispered.

"Miss Morton, I – "

"Sarah."

"Sarah – I – "

"I do so admire a man in uniform," breathed Sarah, putting her head on his shoulder. "So dashing. So exciting . . ."

"Sarah," croaked Ponsonby, "I feel that I must – "

"Do you know that you have the most beautiful eyebrows I've ever seen, Percival?" purred Sarah.

Without warning, she fell back on the chaise, pulling the confused young man so that he sprawled on top of her. The door opened and Jack strode into the room and slammed it behind him. Ponsonby struggled to sit up.

Jack, very stiff and correct in his lieutenant's uniform, glared at the young man as if speechless.

"*Nelson!*" squeaked Sarah.

"*Who?*" gasped Ponsonby.

"Who the devil are you, sir?" rasped Jack, clasping his hands behind his back and sticking out his chin truculently.

Ponsonby was too confused to speak.

"*Stand up!*" roared Jack. Ponsonby leapt to his feet.

"Scott-Ponsonby," he muttered.

Jack looked him up and down as if he was a piece of furniture he intended to buy.

"So," he said finally, "Scott-Ponsonby, eh? Well, my name is Sharpley, sir. Nelson Sharpley – and I require an immediate explanation of your scandalous conduct!"

Ponsonby gaped. "Scandalous?" he stammered.

"What else would you call it?" asked Jack with icy politeness.

"I assure you, lieutenant – "

"I find you forcing your attentions on my betrothed. Ain't that scandalous?"

"You are mistaken," said Ponsonby hotly.

"Do you think I am blind!" roared Jack. "*I saw you!*"

Ponsonby glared back at him. "What you saw was an accident."

"An *accident?*"

"Miss Morton will tell you – !"

"So you'd hide behind a lady's skirts, would you?" sneered Jack.

113

"Don't insult me, sir!" blazed Ponsonby.

"How could I?" countered Jack.

"The lady knows that I – "

"Keep the lady out of it, Ponsonby," Jack cut in. "Haven't you a shred of honour?"

"My honour isn't in question, sir!" Ponsonby shouted furiously.

"Well I say it is!" countered Jack.

The unfairness of it all was too much for Ponsonby. He lost his temper completely and shouted: "Ask the lady, sir! Ask the lady!"

Jack gripped his sword-hilt. "Do you dare to infer Miss Morton's to blame?" he said coldly.

At this, Sarah burst into tears and threw herself on the chaise longue, sobbing bitterly.

"Blacken her character, would you?" snarled Jack, looking at Ponsonby as if he had just crawled out from under a stone. "To save your own pathetic reputation?"

"*Hear me out!*" shouted Ponsonby at the top of his voice.

"*Hear you out*! Goddam you, you coward – I *call* you out!" And with this, Jack struck the young man swiftly on each cheek with his glove.

Ponsonby went white. "I'll kill you for that!" he whispered, shaking with rage.

"Will you?" smiled Jack. "We'll see!"

"No, Nelson!" sobbed Sarah, falling to her knees.

"Be quiet, madam," said Jack stripping off his jacket.

"Where?" asked Ponsonby, following suit.

"The courtyard," said Jack.

The two of them divested themselves of their sword-belts and drew the swords from their scabbards. Ponsonby bowed. "After you," he said.

Jack returned his bow. "No. After you."

The young lieutenant stalked out of the sitting room,

with a final glare at Sarah and Jack followed him, giving her a wink of triumph. So far his plan had worked perfectly.

Out in the courtyard, the two duellists took up their positions and came on guard. Then they circled, watching each other carefully.

"You're a fool, Mr Sharpley," Ponsonby told Jack. "I'll cut you to ribbons."

He attacked, and Jack knew immediately that the younger man was a fine swordsman. After he had parried a bewilderingly fast combination of cuts and thrusts, Jack locked swords with his opponent in order to find out just how strong he was. With the courtyard wall behind him, he found the necessary leverage to push Ponsonby away quite easily. But the young lieutenant came back at him immediately, and Jack was forced to retreat.

They circled again and were each seeking an opening when Captain Konig, with Sarah on his arm, stormed into the courtyard.

"Put up your swords!" he commanded.

They turned towards him and lowered their weapons.

"Is this how you repay our hospitality, Lieutenant Ponsonby?" snapped Captain Konig.

"He challenged me!" answered Ponsonby indignantly.

"He forced his attentions on Sarah!" Jack interrupted.

"That's a lie!"

"Be silent!" said Captain Konig. "This is my house, sir! My home! I won't tolerate such barbarity. Brother officers brawling like street ruffians! Your uncle shall hear of this, young man, I promise you!"

Ponsonby was aghast. "No, Captain Konig, I – " he began.

"He shall, I say!" the captain went on. "Do you think I can ignore this outrage? You have brought dishonour on yourself and on the navy. And I intend you shall be punished for it. Come Sarah!"

With a final cold stare at Ponsonby, Captain Konig turned on his heel and took Sarah back into the house.

Ponsonby was sweating, but not from the exertion. "My God, if he informs my uncle – !"

Jack chuckled. "Oh, he will," he assured the young man. "You can count on it. And duelling's a court martial matter."

"It takes two to fight a duel," said Ponsonby nastily.

"Yes, but you're forgetting," said Jack. "I'm betrothed to his grand-daughter. And that means that his account of the fray will be somewhat one-sided, I'd imagine!"

"The hypocrite!" Ponsonby burst out. "The disgrace will ruin me! My father will cut me off with a shilling! I'll be barred from every club in London!"

Jack shrugged. "It ain't the end of the world," he said casually. "Perhaps the army would have you."

"I wish in Heaven I'd never come to this accursed house!" Ponsonby wailed.

Jack put his hand on the distracted lieutenant's shoulder. "Kismet, Ponsonby," he said gravely.

"Eh?" said Ponsonby, who lacked a classical education.

"Fate," Jack explained. He paused reflectively. "Mind you – there could be a way out of this."

"Could there?" asked Ponsonby eagerly.

Jack scratched his head. "Though why *I* should help *you* – "

"Go on – "

Jack leant against the water-butt. "The old man dotes on Sarah. She's the apple of his eye. Now if I *coax* her, she might be persuaded to make him change his mind. Not write to your uncle, you understand. You apologise, and he forgives you; and we shake hands and the whole affair's forgotten."

Ponsonby stared at him. "You really think that's possible?" he said hoarsely.

"Perhaps," said Jack lightly. "But you must give me your word not to come bothering the girl again."

"I tell you I have no designs on Miss Morton," replied Ponsonby, flaring up again.

"Your word, lieutenant," said Jack coldly.

Ponsonby nodded. "You have it."

As the two of them moved back into the house, Jack paused. "There's something else," he said softly.

"What's that?" said Ponsonby.

"I was told last night you are holding a lad at your rendezvous. A Welsh boy."

"What of it?"

"I want him released."

Ponsonby was astounded. "Released?"

Jack gave him a hard look. "He's under age and you know it. Besides, he works for – a friend of mine."

"No!" the lieutenant said petulantly. "Damnation, why should I?"

Jack smiled at him. "Because of your Rear-Admiral uncle," he said slowly.

The thought of his uncle decided the young man, and he nodded his agreement. "But only if Captain Konig forgets the whole business," he said.

"Oh, he will," Jack smiled. "I'm sure of it!"

The whole charade had been a great success, and now Jack had Lieutenant Ponsonby just where he wanted him. After a touching scene, during which Ponsonby apologised and was forgiven by Captain Konig, the two officers shook hands and set off to The Raven to release Honesty Evans.

As they approached the inn, the coxswain could be

heard trying to drum up a few genuine recruits from a little circle of onlookers.

"Will you stand by and let Bonaparte and his murdering cut-throats set foot on British soil?" he asked them rhetorically. "We have the finest navy in the world, mates. Honour and glory and plenty of booze. And we welcome all true blue Englishmen who will fight for liberty."

During this arrant piece of hypocrisy, Jack and Ponsonby pushed their way through the crowd and went inside the inn. The coxswain continued to harangue his audience, never giving a sign that he had recognised a man he had once served under: Jack Vincent!

Inside The Raven, some of the press gang sat playing cards. They leapt to their feet and saluted the two lieutenants.

"Fetch the Welsh lad!" ordered Ponsonby. He turned to the serving girl. "Two tankards of ale!" he snapped.

Jack sat down with his back to the door, and failed to see the coxswain peer in and beckon to Ponsonby.

"That lieutenant, sir – " he whispered as his officer came to him. "I know him!"

"His name's Sharpley," said Ponsonby.

The coxswain shook his head. "No it ain't," he said quietly. "It's Vincent. Jack Vincent."

Lieutenant Ponsonby's eyes narrowed.

"And he's no lieutenant, neither," the coxswain continued. " 'Cos I served with him – right up to the Court of Inquiry when he resigned his commission."

"When was this?" whispered Ponsonby.

"Three years ago," said the coxswain. "Afore he turned smuggler."

At this moment, Honesty was dragged into the taproom and Jack turned to face him.

"Mister Jack!" gasped Honesty.

Ponsonby advanced grimly. "Mister Jack?" he mocked. "Would that be Mister Jack Vincent?"

Jack sprang to his feet, drawing his sword. He recognised the coxswain and knew that his pretence was over.

"Higgins!" he smiled. "I didn't know you without your beard!"

Ponsonby also drew. "Take the boy back!" he shouted.

Jack covered the door. "*Run!*" he yelled to Honesty.

Honesty raced out, and Jack kicked the door shut behind his back. The sailors rushed towards him, but Ponsonby barked: "Leave him to me!" and they stopped in their tracks.

"We've unfinished business," said Ponsonby with menace.

"Ah yes," drawled Jack. " '*Into ribbons*', wasn't it?"

Ponsonby thrust at him and Jack parried, holding his ground in front of the door. Ponsonby broke off the attack while Jack waited calmly for his next move. Again the young lieutenant came at him, but nothing he could do could move Jack from the door. Honesty had a good start by now, and everyone in the taproom knew it.

"Why don't you call it quits, Ponsonby?" said Jack with a grin. "You'll never catch him now."

"Then I'll take you instead," replied the lieutenant.

But as he leapt in, Jack counter-attacked, taking him by surprise. He drove Ponsonby across the inn so fast that he almost lost his balance. The two of them circled, while the sailors watched, enthralled by the contest. The duellists swapped cut and thrust in the centre of the room, and this time Ponsonby was the first to break off.

"You're not quite as good as you think you are!" Jack told him calmly. This sally provoked Ponsonby into a wild attack as it was intended to do, and although he drove Jack back, he was no longer in control. The smuggler flicked the sword from Ponsonby's hand and pointed his own blade at the young man's throat.

"Tell 'em to back off!"

Ponsonby could see that Jack meant business.

"Do as he says," he gasped.

"Everyone's cutlass on the deck!" Jack commanded.

There was a clatter of weapons as the men obeyed. Jack hurled Ponsonby's sword upwards and it quivered into a roof beam. Then he backed carefully to the door, keeping his sword within half an inch of the terrified lieutenant's neck.

"I'd forget the whole business, if I were you, Ponsonby," he chuckled. "Unless, of course, you would prefer to be the laughing stock of the British Navy!"

Jack pushed him towards the press gang and was out of the door in a flash. The coxswain and the others rushed at it, but Lieutenant Ponsonby stopped them.

The thought that Jack might tell everyone how he'd been made a fool of, and the possibility that it might reach his uncle's ears, filled him with dread: he couldn't bear to be laughed at. So he swallowed his pride and accepted the fact that he had been out-manœuvred by a better man.

CHAPTER NINE

BY the end of the week the press gang's work had finished and the men they had culled from the Quayhaven borough were taken to the receiving ship at Farnmouth and signed on in His Majesty's Navy. Lieutenant Scott-Ponsonby was commended for his keenness and ability; the Union Jack no longer flew over The Raven's door; and the smugglers of the district breathed again. The deadly game of hide-and-seek with the Excise men was resumed once again.

One day, when Jack was plodding over the sand-dunes in driving rain, he saw three masked riders pursuing another man across the beach. As he watched, the hunted man was pulled from his horse. He was on his feet in a moment, and breaking free, whipped out his cutlass and began defending himself vigorously. But the odds against him were too great and Jack could see that it was only a matter of time before the man was killed.

He raced across the dunes to his aid, and between them they began to beat back the three ruffians, who, deciding they'd had enough, remounted their horses and galloped away down the beach.

Jack sheathed his sword, and the little man did the same. Then he took a snuff-box from his pocket, opened it and held it out to Jack, who took a pinch of snuff and handed it back politely. The little man inhaled a large pinch of snuff, brushed his fingers against his coat, snapped the box shut and put it back in his pocket.

"So you were in the navy," he said, in a Scottish accent.

"Why do you say that?" Jack replied, somewhat taken aback.

"Tah, mon!" snorted the man, "that's obvious from the style of your bladework!"

He turned and walked back to his horse and began looking it over. "My name's Arrow," he said briefly.

Jack nodded. "I know your name."

Mr Arrow appeared satisfied that his horse was sound, and straightened up with a sigh of relief. He eyed Jack enigmatically. "D'you know my occupation?" he asked.

"You're a shark," Jack replied.

Mr Arrow pursed his lips and looked quite sour. "An unfortunate appellation," he said. "I prefer Excise Officer, Mr Vincent."

It was Jack's turn to be surprised, and Arrow noted this. "Oh, yes, I know *your* name, and – er – your occupation."

"I'm a fisherman," said Jack evenly.

Arrow gave a short, hard laugh.

"Will you take a drink with me, Mr Arrow?" Jack asked politely.

"Na, na, I canna drink with a – *fisherman*," said Arrow dourly as he swung himself into the saddle. Then he leant forward and said: "A word of warning, Mr Vincent. I've been sent here for a purpose. Tae sweep smuggling from this coast. Those villains want to stop me but I'm damn near tae doin' it. So you'd best keep to your fishing, mon!" A faint smile crossed his features, and he held out his hand. "My grateful thanks, Mr Vincent," he said.

Jack took his hand and they shook; then the Excise man turned his horse and galloped off down the beach.

The heavy rain, which had been sweeping across the dunes, had slackened when Jack reached the cliff path, and by the time he climbed to the top, the sun was shining again and he could see the distant chimneys of Westmore Hall. He set out across the glistening moor.

At the Hall, Sir Paul Fisher, a tall handsome man, was walking in the garden with Sarah. Sir Paul was in his late forties and had a worldly, monied air about him. He was indeed extremely rich. Although his coat was plain, the material was of the very finest and the cut showed the hand of a master tailor. He was a landowner with considerable power and authority in the borough: a magistrate and Member of Parliament. He had been a friend of Sarah's family since she was a baby.

"And how is your grandfather?" he asked with a kindly smile.

Sarah sighed. "As difficult as ever," she replied. "But at least his book is finally finished."

"I cannot believe it," chuckled Sir Paul. "He has been writing it ever since I've known him."

"No truly," said Sarah. "It is finished. So he's gone off to London to see his publisher. And then I've no doubt there'll be a round of visits to his old cronies in Tilbury."

"Where the talk will be of ships, and trade and the sea!" said Sir Paul with a laugh.

Sarah nodded. "And precious little else."

They walked through into the rose garden, and then Sir Paul took Sarah's hand and made her sit beside him. "I have a particular reason for this visit," he said gravely. "How long have I known you?"

"Since I was a child," said Sarah.

He looked into her eyes. "You are a child no longer," he said softly. "Now you are a beautiful young woman."

Sarah did her best to lighten the mood. "Dear Paul," she laughed, "you've always flattered me."

The nobleman grasped her hand between his. "No – it's true. And I confess that I've fallen most desperately in love with you."

"Then I am flattered indeed," Sarah replied, a note of alarm creeping into her voice.

"But not displeased?"

"What can I say?" said Sarah, trying hard to remain calm.

"Why, my dear, what you feel," answered Sir Paul. He gazed at her earnestly. "Please – you must be honest. Surely it is not impossible that your friendship for me could deepen into love?"

"Paul – I do love you, but – "

"Yes?"

"But not as *you* would have me love you," Sarah went on, blushing with embarrassment. Sir Paul released her hand and looked away.

"Forgive me," he said sadly. "I've been too hasty."

"No, Paul – "

"I have. The suddenness of my declaration has distressed you – I can see that. Perhaps when you have time to consider – "

"But, Paul, I – "

But he interrupted her. "You need say nothing further. It is enough that you know of my feelings and will allow me to continue in hope."

Sarah had always been very fond of Sir Paul, but his proposal had come as a complete surprise. Never, in her wildest dreams, had she considered marriage to him. So it was something of a relief when Jack vaulted lightly over the fence and walked towards them.

He looked Sir Paul up and down for a moment and then said to Sarah: "Have you seen Honesty?"

Sarah introduced him uncomfortably. "Mr Vincent. Sir Paul Fisher."

Jack bowed. "Your servant," he said before addressing Sarah again. "Well have you?"

Sarah shook her head.

"Then where the devil's he got to?" muttered Jack. "I need him for the boat."

By this time, Sir Paul was beginning to feel out of things, so he smiled at Jack and said: "You are a fisherman?"

"Well done!" replied Jack sarcastically.

Sir Paul stiffened. "You smell like a fisherman."

There was an icy silence, while Jack looked at him; he smiled but his eyes were cold. "And you smell of nothing," he said quietly. "Nothing at all. So what does that make you?" He turned back to Sarah. "If that little scallywag comes to the house, send him to me at once!"

Sir Paul was white with rage. "I am sure that Miss Morton – " he began.

"Miss Morton has her own tongue," said Jack.

"You are a very direct young man," said Sir Paul calmly.

"If you mean rude, say rude," said Jack.

"I said, direct," said Sir Paul, controlling his temper.

"I know damn well what you said," said Jack.

Sir Paul took a deep breath. "I do not intend to quarrel with you, though it would seem you want me to."

Jack stuck his hands in his pockets and smiled. "I don't give a hoot, matey, one or t'other," he mocked.

The two of them looked at each other like a pair of fighting cocks who are just about to tear each to pieces, and then Sir Paul addressed himself to Sarah. "Sarah – I think it is time I bid you goodbye for the present."

"High time, I'd say," said Jack rudely.

Sir Paul ignored him completely. "You will think on what I told you," he asked her softly.

"I will," Sarah replied.

He kissed her hand. "Then that is all I hope for." Once again he turned to Jack. "Sir. Had we been elsewhere, and alone, you would have answered for your impertinence."

"Get back in your box!" Jack replied coolly.

For a moment, Sir Paul Fisher stood quivering with

indignation. Then, without another word, he stalked off towards his carriage which stood in the drive.

"You are insufferable!" Sarah hissed at Jack, and hurried after her outraged suitor. Jack watched with amusement while Sir Paul kissed Sarah's hand again and climbed into his coach. Sarah waved as it moved off, and then came back to Jack with a face like thunder.

"How could you behave so boorishly?" she cried. "Paul is an old friend of mine."

"I could tell that," Jack replied. "The man was positively drooling."

"You insulted him!"

"*He* insulted *me*!"

"I have never been so humiliated!"

"Rubbish! You enjoyed it!"

Sarah looked at Jack. He had several days' growth of beard; his dark hair hung lankly over his frayed collar; and his sea boots were cracked and scuffed.

"Have you any notion who he is?" she said disdainfully.

"No," shrugged Jack. "None."

"Sir Paul Fisher owns most of the County. He has estates in Hanover; he was Colonel in Chief of the Queen's German Regiment; he is a personal friend of the Duke of Cambridge – "

"And he's too old for you," Jack cut in.

Sarah turned crimson. "How dare you!" she gasped.

Jack chuckled. "I'm right, ain't I?" he said. "He wants to marry you, doesn't he?"

"What business is that of yours?" Sarah flung back at him.

"None at all," countered Jack. "If you want to marry a rich old gentleman, that's your affair. The fact that you're really in love with me has nothing to do with it."

Sarah turned on him furiously. "You're so very sure of

yourself, aren't you?" She walked away and quickened her pace as Jack came after her.

"What are you running away from, Sarah?" he said, catching her by the arm.

Sarah shook herself free. "You're a bully," she sobbed, "you're vain, you're arrogant and you're *impossible*!"

She broke from him, seething, and ran into the house. Jack tried to follow her, but the door was slammed in his face.

Silly girl, he thought, and walked away from the house whistling a jaunty air. It was all for Sarah's benefit. Jack knew she would be watching from the window.

A week went by. Jack made a couple of runs to Roscoff, bringing back cargoes of brandy and tobacco which he put in his 'storeroom'. He decided to keep away from Westmore Hall until Sarah had simmered down, so he spent his days making a new bowsprit for the *Mary Jane*. It was a very long bowsprit and quite illegal, enabling him to rig a much larger jib-sail which would give his lugger greater speed and mobility. Only the cutters of the Revenue Service were allowed such bowsprits, so Jack intended making his removable. He would then be able to replace it with one the correct length, if any nosey Customs man wished to inspect the boat.

It was while he was working away with a spokeshave outside the cottage one afternoon, that the familiar figure of Honesty Evans came trudging up the cliff path towards him, whistling a hymn.

Jack pretended to take no notice of the boy, and carried on working. Honesty, who had expected some kind of welcome, was a bit put out. However, he sat himself down on an empty half-anker and addressed his friend cheerfully.

"Morning, Mister Jack," he said. "Any work?"

"There would've been a week ago," Jack answered

without bothering to look up. "Where the devil were you?"

"Ah, well, you see," replied Honesty quickly, "I've been visiting my auntie."

"And which auntie would that be?" said Jack, blowing shavings from the bowsprit.

"Gladys," said Honesty. "The one with the squint and three goats."

Jack carefully put down the spokeshave, straightened up and gave Honesty a long, hard stare. "When did you get back?" he asked slowly.

"Just now!" replied the boy.

"You are a liar!" said Jack.

Honesty stared at him.

"I want that knife back, Honesty," said Jack.

"What knife?"

"Don't play games, boy. My midshipman's dirk."

"Oh, you mean that old dagger you keep on the dresser?" said Honesty. "When did you lose it?"

Jack was now convinced that Honesty was lying. He advanced on him menacingly. "I didn't lose it," he said. "It was stolen yesterday, while I was out fishing. Stolen by a lying, twisting little filcher!"

Jack tried to grab him by the coat, but Honesty was too quick. He hopped off the barrel and out of range.

"I never took it!" he said indignantly. "I couldn't have. I only got back this morning!"

Jack didn't believe him. "If you sold it, you're in for a whipping!"

"If I didn't take it, how could I sell it?" shouted Honesty.

Again Jack tried to grab him, but the boy ran off and eyed the smuggler warily from a distance. The little scene was watched by Mr Arrow as he trotted towards the cottage on his bay mare.

"What's the boy done?" he asked.

E

"He's a thief," Jack explained, loud enough for Honesty to hear.

"Oh no I'm not!" he yelled. "I didn't take your old knife, Mister Jack!" Then he turned and ran away into the bracken.

Jack turned to Arrow. "He'll wait a couple of days and then bring it back, with a tale of how he found the thief and tricked him out of it."

Arrow dismounted.

"What do you want, Mr Arrow?" asked Jack warily. "You haven't come to search, have you?"

Arrow shook his head. "Can we go inside, mon?"

Once inside the cottage, Arrow sat down, took out his snuff-box, opened it and handed it to Jack in silence. Jack took a large pinch of snuff, and handed the box back. Arrow also took a large pinch, and put the snuff-box away. This little ritual over, the Excise man leant forward and looked hard at Jack.

"Can I trust you?"

"Maybe."

"I know you to be a man of honour," said Arrow softly, "despite your present occupation. You saved my life."

Arrow took a large sealed envelope from his coat pocket. "I want you to look after this for me," he said softly. "I'll collect it when I return from London."

Jack gave him a puzzled smile. "What's the mystery?" The little man gave a snort of exasperation.

"There's nae mystery. They want me dead."

"Who do?"

Arrow shook his head. "It's better ye dinnae ken, but if they succeed – open it and act on what you find."

"Then I pray I won't have to," said Jack with a grim smile.

"Amen to that!"

Arrow rose, shook Jack's hand and went to the door.

"After all, I'm a shark, am I not?" he chuckled. "And a shark has an awfu' big bite."

Arrow intended crossing the moor that afternoon, but he had barely travelled the best part of a mile from Jack's cottage when he was ambushed by a gang of masked men. Held between two of them, the Excise man waited calmly as their leader took a naval dirk from his belt. He advanced on Arrow and with a curse, stabbed him to the heart. With a choking cry, the little man fell to the ground and, after a moment, lay still. In silence, the gang remounted and rode off; the sound of their horses' hooves died away like the beating of distant drums.

The next morning a party of dragoons rode up to the cottage with Honesty Evans. The sergeant-in-charge burst in on Jack without ceremony and threw the naval dirk so that it quivered into the table in front of him.

"Is it yours?" barked the sergeant.

Jack looked at him steadily. "I'm not a midshipman," he said quietly.

"Bring in the boy!" ordered the sergeant.

Honesty was dragged into the cottage.

"We met him on the road," explained the sergeant. "Showed him that dirk. He says it's yours."

Honesty, who knew nothing of Arrow's murder, looked at Jack and said: "You see, I hadn't stolen it, Mister Jack! Where did you find it?" he asked the sergeant.

"You know where, don't you, Vincent?" said the sergeant. "I'm arresting you for the murder of Excise Officer William Arrow."

It was pointless to resist. Jack stood mutely while he was manacled and led outside.

The dragoons took him to Farnmouth Castle, the headquarters of their regiment. It was a gloomy pile, dominating the headland to the west of the port. Here, Jack was locked in a tower and, eventually granted an interview with Lieutenant-Colonel Ward, the garrison commander.

Ward was a pink-faced, thick-set man who reminded Jack of a rather sleepy pig. He glared at Jack, and asked him if he intended to confess.

"Not when I'm innocent," Jack answered him.

"You'll have the chance to prove that at your trial," sneered Ward.

"I didn't kill Arrow," said Jack, doing his best to control his temper. "Dammit, I helped the man when he was attacked last week."

Ward looked at him with amusement. "You must think me very gullible, sir," he said. "A smuggler help an Excise man? That don't seem very likely to me! I suggest you tried to bribe him. And that when he arrested you – you killed him."

"Rubbish!"

Lieutenant-Colonel Ward was not used to prisoners who answered back. "Then can you explain why he was found less than a mile from your cottage. With a naval dirk in his ribs that the Evans boy identified as yours?"

"That dirk had been stolen from me," said Jack. "He'll tell you so."

"Oh, I'm sure he will," drawled Ward sarcastically. "Especially now he knows of the murder."

This was a difficult one for Jack. "Very well," he said quickly, "then tell me this. Why should I leave it in the body?"

"A midshipman's dirk is common enough," said Ward dismissively. "There must be thousands of them. Except we've found out this was yours. Do you deny it?"

Jack remained silent. There was no point in denying it. The dirk was his; but who had taken it, and had killed Arrow with it, remained a complete mystery.

The news of Jack's arrest spread like wildfire. Sarah learnt of it from Sir Paul Fisher, who tried hard to comfort her. In spite of her quarrel with Jack she found it impossible to accept that he could be a murderer.

"I *can't* believe it! *I can't*!" she sobbed.

"You care for this man, don't you?" said Sir Paul gently. "Do you love him?"

Sarah stared out of the window. The moor stretched away into the distance, its horizon shrouded in mist.

"I don't know," she said slowly. "But I care what happens to him. I care very much." She smiled ruefully. "Oh, I know he's a difficult man. He's like the sea; stormy and gentle by turns, and whenever we part I never know when I'll see him again, or what he'll say to me when we do meet."

There was silence for a moment, and then she said: "Do you think he killed that man?"

Sir Paul shook his head sadly. "It hardly matters what I think, my dear. Vincent is a known smuggler, and you say he's unpredictable."

"But do you, Paul?" persisted Sarah.

Sir Paul frowned, and paused before he replied. "Such a nature can make a man very dangerous," he said finally. "You've seen him angry, Sarah. Be honest; were you not frightened by it?"

Sarah's eyes filled with tears, and Sir Paul took her in his arms for protection and comfort.

Meanwhile, Honesty Evans, looking somewhat fatter than usual, approached the gatehouse of Farnmouth Castle where he was challenged by the guard.

"What do you want?" said the guard, a thin spotty youth not much older than Honesty himself.

"I've come to see Mister Vincent," replied Honesty.

"Have you indeed!" laughed the guard. "Well you can't."

"It ain't your blessed castle!" retorted Honesty cheekily.

They were joined by the sergeant who had captured Jack. Honesty decided to try a different tack.

"Mister Vincent's been like a father to me, sir," he said, managing to squeeze a tear from each eye. "I've nobody, I haven't – nobody but him. If they hang him, I'll be all alone again without having the chance to say goodbye. Now, you wouldn't want that on your conscience, would you?" He burst into tears.

"Don't blub, lad," said the sergeant uncomfortably. "It ain't manly."

Honesty gave a convincing performance of pulling himself together. "You're right, sir," he sniffed. "I mustn't give way. It's kind of you to take any notice of me at all. I mean if I hadn't recognised that old dagger, you wouldn't have got him, would you?"

The sergeant nodded. The boy's evidence had certainly made things easier.

"Only five minutes, sir," Honesty pleaded.

The guard tittered, and the sergeant glared at him. "Sergeant," he told Honesty. "Only hofficers is 'sir'."

"Please, sergeant," Honesty asked politely.

The sergeant relented. There could be no harm in letting the lad see the prisoner. He called to another of his men, who escorted Honesty to the tower where Jack was imprisoned.

"Well, Mister Jack, how have you been keeping?" said Honesty cheerfully, after the door closed and they were left alone.

Jack looked at him in astonishment as the boy took a file from his pocket, undid his coat and uncoiled a length of rope from his middle.

"Have they been treating you all right?" he said loudly for the benefit of the soldiers outside. Then he came close to Jack and whispered: "All you gotta do, see, is file

135

through one of those bars, climb down this rope and run for it. I'll be waiting among the trees."

The door was thrown open. "That's what you think!" said the guard who'd been watching through the spy-hole. Honesty's escort stood beside him.

"Get rid of this object," the guard told him.

"Ain't you going to arrest me?" asked Honesty indignantly.

"Not if I can help it!" said the guard.

The dragoon was dragging Honesty out of the cell when Jack remembered the papers Arrow had left with him. He shouted to Honesty: "See you wind the clock and *take it to Sarah*!"

Honesty looked at him in bewilderment.

"Get him out of here!" growled the guard.

Honesty was marched back to the gatehouse and sent on his way with a well-aimed kick. He picked himself off the road and swore at the soldiers in Welsh.

Jack's command puzzled him all the way to the cottage. But when he found the large envelope sticking out from behind the clock, he knew at once this was what he was supposed to take to Sarah.

There was a sound outside: someone was opening the door very carefully. He ducked down behind the table and the door swung open. Sarah stood on the threshold.

"Honesty?" she said softly. "Are you here?"

Honesty got to his feet with an embarrassed smile.

"I hoped I'd find you here," said Sarah with relief. "Have you any news?"

"I've been up to the castle, Miss Sarah," said Honesty quickly. "I tried to get him out, but my daring plan was foiled."

"Do you believe he did it?"

"He couldn't have done it. He'd lost that knife the day before."

"Lost it?" questioned Sarah. "Perhaps it had been stolen."

"Of course it had been stolen," sighed Honesty impatiently. "To kill that man Arrow." He held out the packet of papers. "Here – I reckon Mister Jack wants you to have this."

Sarah took it from him and tore open the envelope. Inside was another with a note folded round it.

"What's it say?" asked Honesty.

Sarah unfolded the note and began to read aloud.

" 'My dear Vincent, it is strange to write this letter knowing that if you read it I shall already be a dead man. But if justice is to be served and the truth known, there is now no other way. Therefore, I ask you to deliver this in person to a Captain Tennant at the Admiralty in London. Godspeed and good fortune. William Arrow.' "

She looked up at Honesty with her eyes shining with excitement. The note alone was enough to prove Jack innocent.

"But what's in here?" asked Honesty, picking up the other envelope.

"Something worth killing for," said Sarah snatching it back.

She ran outside and mounted her horse. Honesty called to her: "Where are you going?"

"To someone who can help us!" cried Sarah.

Paul would help her, she thought. He had power and influence; and with Arrow's letter as evidence, would quickly obtain Jack's release.

It was eight miles to Ellingford House – Sir Paul's country estate – and by the time Sarah reached it, her horse was wet with sweat. She ran into the pillared hall and called excitedly. After a moment Sir Paul appeared, puzzled to see her so distraught; he led her to his library without a word.

"But this is *fantastic*!" he said after having read Arrow's letter. "This means your Mr Vincent is no murderer. Where did you find it?"

"In Jack's cottage," Sarah told him.

Sir Paul took her by the shoulder. "Forgive me, Sarah," he said quietly. "Perhaps I wanted to believe him guilty."

"You will use your influence to see that he is released?" she said eagerly.

Sir Paul smiled warmly. "My dear," he said, "I will see that the accusation of murder is dropped. But the man is still a smuggler. However, I will do what I can. Now where is the other document Arrow mentioned?"

Sarah handed it to him, and Sir Paul broke the seal and read it carefully. Finally, he looked up at Sarah and said: "This must go to London at once. It seems that Mr Arrow had discovered that certain Revenue officers are taking bribes; even working with the smuggling gangs."

"So that was why he was killed," gasped Sarah. "But why did they try to blame Jack for it?"

Sir Paul shrugged. "I must act on this immediately," he went on. "We must ensure that Arrow has not died in vain, and Colonel Ward must be informed that Vincent is no murderer."

Sir Paul ushered Sarah to the door.

"Return home, Sarah," he smiled. "You may rest assured that I will do everything I can."

Sarah turned in the doorway, put her arms around him and kissed him warmly. He watched her as she ran lightly across the hall, then he closed the door.

"She's gone," he said quietly.

Colonel Ward stepped out from the adjoining room and Sir Paul handed him Arrow's letter. "This will upset you!"

he said grimly. "You see, Colonel, your name heads the list."

"By God, he'd uncovered the whole organisation," said Ward, after a few minutes. He looked at Sir Paul. "Only your name is missing."

"But for how long, if this reached London?" snarled Sir Paul, snatching back the letter. "We'd have Customs Commissioners by the boatload, prying into every corner, asking awkward questions. It is fortunate Sarah brought me this."

"But what will she think if Vincent comes to trial?" asked Ward anxiously.

"That's true," muttered Sir Paul. He sat down slowly at his desk and his eyes narrowed as he pondered the problem. At last a smile came to his lips, and he nodded to himself, approving his own cleverness.

"I suggest that before Arrow's note reaches you to establish Vincent's innocence," he said, looking hard at Ward, "he is killed attempting to escape."

Colonel Ward was horrified. Arrow's murder had already appalled him. Now he was being told to arrange another. He shook his head violently.

"I cannot be a party to it!" he said.

Sir Paul slowly tore up Arrow's letter to Jack and threw the pieces in the fire.

"My dear Ward," he said softly, "you will do as I say or we will all go under!"

CHAPTER TEN

AFTER seeing Sarah ride off, Honesty had gone up to Farnmouth Castle where he hoped to get a message to Jack. He wanted him to know that he'd found Arrow's letters and that, with any luck, he would soon be free. But when the sergeant saw him approaching the gatehouse, he threatened him with a thrashing.

Honesty stood his ground. "I've got a message for Mister Jack," he said.

"And half a keg of gunpowder in your pocket, I wouldn't wonder!" growled the sergeant, eyeing him suspiciously. "Push off, lad, afore you feel my boot."

"Well, will you tell him – "

"I'll tell him nothing," snapped the sergeant. "Get away from here, you young imp!"

"The last time I saw a mouth like yours," said Honesty angrily, "it had a fish hook in it!"

The sergeant lumbered towards him, and Honesty darted off like lightning.

But he didn't go far. When the sergeant returned inside the gatehouse, Honesty circled round to some bushes growing in the deep gully that had once been a water-filled moat. He wanted to be the first one to welcome Jack when he was released.

After a moment, Colonel Ward rode up to the gatehouse and the sergeant hurried out and saluted.

"I've learnt there may be an attempt to rescue the prisoner," said Colonel Ward. Honesty pricked up his ears.

"There's been one already, sir," grinned the sergeant. "The Evans boy brought a rope and a file!"

"A serious attempt," said the colonel grimly. "If Vincent breaks out, he forfeits the right to my protection, and is to be shot on sight."

The sergeant frowned. "An unarmed man, sir? But that – "

"*On sight*, sergeant," snapped the colonel and rode through the gatehouse towards the castle.

Honesty was puzzled. Who could possibly intend rescuing Jack, and how had the colonel discovered it?

While he was doing his best to think it out, a stranger rode up to the gatehouse. He was a weatherbeaten man, with sharp eyes and an air of authority. The guard challenged him, and called to the sergeant.

"I wish to see the commander of the garrison," the stranger said crisply.

"Your name, sir?" asked the sergeant.

"Vincent," the man replied.

From his hiding place, Honesty stared in amazement. Could he be Jack's brother?

"Dismount, sir!" ordered the sergeant. The man obeyed instantly.

"Your sword, sir," said the sergeant.

"Is that necessary?"

"Yes, sir, it is."

"Very well," he said, and unbuckling his sword belt, he handed it to the sergeant, who ordered one of his men to escort the visitor to the colonel.

Honesty watched the dragoons and the mysterious Mr Vincent walk through the gatehouse to the main gate of the castle.

Colonel Ward was surprised to see a relative of his prisoner, and was determined to get rid of the man as soon as possible. He had no intention of letting him see Vincent. Such a meeting could ruin his plan. But he smiled at his visitor politely and asked him how he could help.

141

"I understand my brother is being held here," said the man.

"Aye, sir," Ward replied smoothly. "For the murder of William Arrow, a Riding Officer of the Excise Service. He was killed with a naval dirk. We have proof that it belonged to your brother. He was in the navy, I believe."

"He was."

"And then court-martialled?"

"No, sir. He resigned his commission."

Ward grimaced at this. The difference between resigning and being thrown out was obviously lost on him.

"My purpose in coming here is not to discuss my brother's character," the other went on, "or even the circumstances of his arrest, but to ask why *you* have him *here*?"

Ward cleared his throat uneasily. "Because he was arrested by my men," he said finally.

"Then when will he be transferred to the civil authority?"

"When it's convenient," snapped Ward.

"This is monstrous!"

"No, sir. It's the law!"

The weather-beaten man looked at Ward. "I would like to see him."

"That's impossible," Ward replied flatly.

"Why so?"

"Because I do not wish it!"

Mr Vincent pulled on his gloves, put on his hat and turned to go.

"I shall take up this matter with the Lord Lieutenant," he said coldly.

"By all means do so, Mr Vincent," Ward replied, very relieved to have got rid of him so easily. "But let me tell you this. My regiment works closely with the Revenue Service; as does the Royal Navy. It's common knowledge

that your brother's a smuggler; and with the present
evidence against him, I have every right to hold him here.
Good day to you, sir!"

Ward's visitor was taken back to the gatehouse, and his
sword was returned to him. The sergeant could tell he was
very angry. Colonel Ward had obviously sent him away
with a flea in his ear. He remounted his horse and, with a
curt nod, trotted away without another word.

Honesty waited a few minutes, and then ran down the
road after him. He cut through the woods and managed to
intercept the stranger just as he was trotting off in the
direction of Quayhaven.

"Mr Vincent!" he called. "Mr Vincent!"

The rider reined his horse and looked sharply at him.

"Who are you?" he asked warily.

"A friend of your brother's," Honesty told him. "They
know all about your plan at the castle."

"What plan? What d'ye mean, boy?"

"The escape plan," went on Honesty impatiently. "They
mean to shoot Mister Jack. I heard the colonel tell them
to."

Mr Vincent seemed to size up the situation in a moment.

"We're going back," he snapped curtly, and with
Honesty trotting alongside, turned his horse towards
Farnmouth Castle again.

Outside Jack's cell, Ward watched from the shadows as
the guards took in his evening meal. The evening sunlight
slanted in through the narrow window. Jack sniffed at the
unappetising mess in the tin bowl in front of him.

"What's that?" he asked with a look of disgust.

"You'll have to ask the cook, my lad," replied one of
the guards. "But I doubt if he could tell you. By the by,
your brother's been."

"My brother?" repeated Jack in astonishment.

143

"The colonel wouldn't let him see you, though," the guard went on.

Jack stared at the tin bowl. As far as he knew, he had no brother. Absentmindedly he took a spoonful of food and its foul taste made him gag. The guards left the cell; as they passed Colonel Ward they saluted.

Ward waited until they were out of sight and then tiptoed to the cell door. He eased open the peep-hole and peered in at Jack. Then, very carefully, he unlocked the cell door.

Jack heard the key turn in the lock and listened as Ward's footsteps receded. He went quickly to the door and opened it. Who was his mysterious benefactor?

He left the cell, closing the door quietly behind him, and moved silently down the steps, every nerve tense, ready for action. Suddenly, he heard the guards returning, and he flattened himself against the wall. As they appeared round the corner, he launched himself at them and sent one of them reeling back with a savage blow. The other guard raised his musket, and Jack grabbed it by the barrel, pulled the man forward, and kicked his legs from under him. He sprawled over the body of his companion, as Jack pulled the musket from his grasp.

Down the steps he ran, and out into the courtyard. He looked across to the main gate of the castle; from the tower behind him the guards gave the alarm. He heard running feet and a party of dragoons appeared through an archway. He fired, and a howl went up from one of them; the rest flung themselves to the ground.

He made for the main gate amid a hail of bullets. The guards saw him coming and they, too, tried to bring him down, but the darkness, coupled with the speed of his charge, took them by surprise and their bullets whined harmlessly over his head.

Jack reversed his musket and swung it like a club. It

144

caught one of them on the temple and he crashed down unconscious. Jack drove the butt hard into another man's midriff, and raced out of the gate.

The alarm bell was clanging loudly as he sped to the gatehouse, but he could see the sergeant and his men had already pulled shut the gates and were kneeling in front of them, aiming at him.

He swerved and made for the outer wall. He leapt up and clung grimly to the top. The rough stones gave him a foothold, and he clawed his way over and tumbled down into the bushes of the gully.

"This way, Mister Jack!" hissed a familiar voice. "Hurry!"

Honesty and the mysterious stranger led the way down the gully with Jack panting after them. Already soldiers with torches were streaming from the gatehouse. The fugitives crashed on through the undergrowth and found themselves heading for the cliffs. Ahead of them lay the sea.

Jack, whose smuggling activities often brought him near Farnmouth, led his companions along the cliff-top and down a narrow path between gorse bushes on to the rocks below.

The climb down the rocks to the beach would have been dangerous enough in daylight; to attempt it in the dark was madness. But there was no alternative. Already, Colonel Ward's dragoons could be see above them, outlined against the night sky.

Jack led the way down, agile as any mountain goat and Honesty and the stranger followed him as best they could. Bullets whined round them in the darkness, smacking against the rocks like angry bees, but none of the soldiers dared to follow them. At last, drenched in sweat, their hands torn and bleeding, they reached the foreshore. Jack looked curiously at the stranger.

"Who the devil are you?" he gasped.

Honesty gaped. Didn't Mister Jack know his own brother?

"My name's Tennant," the man replied, "I'm a colleague of Mr Arrow's. When he failed to report, we guessed he'd been silenced. He told us of the first attempt on his life, and how you'd helped save him."

Then Honesty told Jack of Arrow's letter and how he had given it with the other documents to Sarah.

"We'll talk later," said Jack. "There's a good hiding place a couple of miles from here. We must reach it before those dragoons pluck up enough courage to follow us."

Jack led them along the shore until they reached a narrow opening in the cliffs, behind which was a fair-sized cave. The back of this cave became a rocky tunnel which led up to the top of the cliff.

"I want you to go to Sarah," Jack told Honesty urgently. "Tell her we're in Hangman's Cave. Bring Arrow's letters!"

The boy nodded, climbed up into the darkness and disappeared from view.

After some minutes, he emerged like a bewildered badger from a rocky hole among the bracken and stared up at the stars. After getting his bearings, he gulped in the cool night air for a moment or two, and then set off across country towards Westmore Hall.

He ran steadily, conserving his strength, and only slowed down when the rising ground forced him to. The moor was a mysterious place at night, and it seemed almost to breathe as the wind blew through the heather.

He crossed a stream, pausing only to scoop up a mouthful of icy water, and stumbled onwards. He could see the Hall now; there were lights shining out into the darkness. Suddenly, he no longer felt tired and quickened his pace.

He let himself in at the side door and was hurrying

146

towards the dining room when Sarah's maid, Jenny, appeared.

"What do you think you're doing?" she said sharply.

"I've got to see Miss Sarah," gasped Honesty. "It's to do with Mister Jack!"

But when he was ushered into the dining room he was surprised to find that Sarah was not alone. There was a richly dressed stranger with her. It was Sir Paul.

"Did you see Mr Vincent?" asked Sarah eagerly. Honesty looked doubtfully at Sir Paul.

"It's – it's private, Miss Sarah," he said.

Sarah smiled. "You can speak freely," she said. "Sir Paul is a friend. He knows everything."

Sir Paul looked hard at the boy. "Is something wrong?" he asked.

Honesty remained silent.

"Don't be frightened," coaxed Sarah. "Sir Paul is going to help Mister Jack."

"There's no need," said Honesty finally. "He's escaped."

Sir Paul, who was expecting the news of Jack's death, stared at Honesty uncomprehendingly.

"They tried to shoot him down," the boy went on, his eyes shining with excitement, "but he got clean away!"

"The fool! The fool!" cried Sir Paul, trying hard to hide his anger. "Why would he do such a thing?"

"He wants to prove his innocence," said Sarah.

"And find the real murderer," added Honesty.

"But the law will do that," said Sir Paul with exasperation. "He must give himself up. If the soldiers find him now – "

"They won't find him," said Honesty calmly.

"Where is he?" asked Sir Paul steadily.

Honesty looked at him. He didn't know this man, and intuitively didn't trust him.

"Please, Honesty!" said Sarah.

"Hangman's Cave," said Honesty reluctantly.

"I'll go to him," said Sarah. "I'll tell him about Arrow's letter!"

"Yes, but not tonight," frowned Sir Paul. "Patrols will be out looking for him; if they follow you – "

Sarah nodded. She would wait until the search was called off.

"You're a good friend, Paul," she said softly.

Sir Paul kissed her hand. "And now I must leave you," he murmured. "Remember, while Vincent is at liberty, his life is in danger."

But when he rode away from the Hall, Sir Paul took the Farnmouth road. He was furious with Colonel Ward; the man was a bungler allowing Vincent to escape: however, there was still time to put matters right.

Ward was in his office when Sir Paul strode in and angrily confronted him.

" 'Shot while trying to escape'," sneered Sir Paul sarcastically. "Really, Ward, your incompetence is breathtaking!"

"He had the devil's own luck!" retorted Ward. "We'll find him!"

"You will," said Sir Paul. "In Hangman's Cave!"

"How do you know?" gasped Ward.

"See to it now," snapped Sir Paul. "I want him dead!"

Meanwhile, in the cave, Jack and Captain Tennant waited for Honesty to return.

"You're not an Excise man, are you, Tennant?" said Jack quietly.

Tennant looked at him with a half smile and shook his head. "Let us say that I am a half-pay captain, working for the Crown," he said mysteriously. "The Customs Commissioners asked us to investigate corruption in the Revenue Service. So Mr Arrow posed as a Excise Officer. But he learnt too much for his safety. Searchers, Collectors

148

and even Port Controllers are all being paid to look the other way, and allow huge cargoes of contraband to be landed. It is bribery and connivance on a vast scale, and we want the man behind it."

"So do I," muttered Jack. "He's probably the one who cooked up the murder charge against me!"

Tennant chuckled. "You should have stayed in the navy," he said quietly. "If you'd kept your temper at that Court of Inquiry, you wouldn't be skulking in this damned cave now."

Jack looked at the mysterious Captain Tennant. "You seem to know a lot about me," he said warily.

Tennant nodded. "I read the report. You deserved that reprimand."

"For sinking a French frigate?"

"For acting against orders, and putting your ship at hazard."

"We were at war! I've never done things by the book."

"We know that," said Captain Tennant.

"Who's we?"

"I can't tell you yet," Tennant replied.

Jack leant forward and when he spoke it was with a bitter intensity. "You want this man, you say. But when you've got him – what then? England's rotten with his kind. Arrogant and merciless men who scorn the poor, and then send them to die in wars that don't concern 'em. Wars to do with power and influence: not with people." Jack stared moodily ahead of him. "And when those wars are won and the poor come home, nothing's changed."

"There'll be war again within the month," Tennant told him.

"How do you know?"

"It's our business to know," Tennant retorted. "Perhaps then you might consider – "

But what Jack was being asked to consider was never

149

revealed, for at that moment there was a sound outside the cave, and Jack put his finger to his lips in warning. He crept forward to the narrow entrance and peered out. Ward and a party of his men were advancing towards the cave.

Jack crept back to Captain Tennant.

"Dragoons," he whispered.

"But who told them?" questioned Tennant. "The boy?"

Jack shook his head, bewildered.

"Who then?"

Jack said nothing. Sarah was the only possible answer. The two men hurried to the back of the cave and began climbing up the narrow tunnel. Below them they could hear Ward calling for Jack to surrender. This was followed by a rattle of musket-fire. As Ward and his men rushed into the cave, Captain Tennant and Jack were scrambling out to safety. By the time the dragoons discovered the tunnel to the cliff-top, the fugitives had disappeared into the night.

CHAPTER ELEVEN

At the Hall, Sarah lay in bed unable to sleep. A dog barked in the courtyard below, and after a moment a sound from the curtained window alerted her. She froze, and suddenly the curtains parted and Jack stood in the moonlight.

"You told them, didn't you?" he said quietly.

"Told them? Told who?" replied Sarah.

"Ward and his men. They knew I was in that cave."

"I swear – "

"They'd have killed me, Sarah. Is that what you want?"

"*No!*"

"No-one else knew," said Jack. "Only you and Honesty – "

"Honesty would never betray – " But there was someone else, thought Sarah. Her friend and erstwhile suitor!

"Paul knew," she told Jack quietly. "Sir Paul Fisher knew."

"Why did you tell him?" asked Jack.

"He's always been a friend," said Sarah. "And he wanted to help. I gave him Arrow's letter. I thought, with his influence, he could – "

"His influence!" exclaimed Jack bitterly. "*He's* the man Tennant's after. Don't you see? He tried to blame me for Arrow's murder, because he was jealous! He wants me out of the way; he considers I'm his rival. And Colonel Ward's his accomplice: he must be. We have them both," he added grimly. Turning to the window, he paused. "I'm sorry I doubted you, Sarah," he said quietly. Then he was gone – as silently as he had come. A moment later Sarah heard a muffled thump as he landed on the terrace below.

Her heart racing, she sat up in bed, filled with horror at what she had heard. The man she had trusted for so many years was corrupt and vicious. He had sought to send an innocent man to the gallows, and was responsible for murder! For the rest of the night she hardly slept, frightened for what Jack might do in revenge.

The following morning, Sir Paul Fisher was at sabre practise in the gardens of his country house at Ellingford. He was anxious to hear the news that Jack Vincent had been killed at Hangman's Cave; and his impatience had driven him to pass the time in action. In front of him stood a dummy made of leather and stuffed with straw. It held a sabre in each of its outstretched arms and as Sir Paul struck at it the dummy would spin round and force him to parry. Absorbed in this strenuous exercise, he failed to see Jack standing only a few feet away, watching him with an amused smile.

"Fisher!"

Sir Paul swung round. Ward had failed again!

"Have they released you?" he asked Jack politely. "I find that hard to believe."

"Someone left the door open," replied Jack. "Or do you find that hard to believe?"

"Almost impossible," said Sir Paul calmly. "So now you're a wanted man."

Jack didn't answer him but came nearer. "Where's Arrow's letter?" he said.

"I really don't know what you're talking about," smiled Sir Paul.

"I think you do," said Jack. "The letter Sarah brought you."

Sir Paul's eyes flickered with fear.

"Oh, yes, I've seen her," Jack went on remorselessly.

"Why else would I be here? She also brought you Arrow's other letter; the one to Captain Tennant in London."

Sir Paul shrugged.

"Where are those letters?" said Jack.

"I thought it better to burn them," replied Sir Paul. "Do you really imagine you can bring me down? Without any evidence?"

" 'The bigger they are – ' "

" 'The harder they fall,' " finished Sir Paul with a sneer. "A very foolish saying. And one without any truth in it."

"Colonel Ward's in your pocket, isn't he?"

Sir Paul smiled at Jack. Perhaps the wretched man could be bribed. "My pocket is a very deep pocket, Mr Vincent," he said carefully.

"It must be."

"I can save your life."

"And buy my silence?"

"Why not?"

Jack flushed angrily.

"You may be able to buy the borough, but you can't buy me!"

Sir Paul chuckled, but his eyes were cold.

"I thought you believed in free trade, Mr Vincent. I thought you were a smuggler. I fail to see the difference between us."

"You're a murderer."

Sir Paul laughed.

"Sarah wouldn't have you, would she?" said Jack softly.

Sir Paul stopped laughing abruptly. He glared venomously at the smuggler and raised his sabre.

"So you chose me for the part of Arrow's killer." Jack drew his sword. "A bad choice, Fisher," he whispered.

"That has become very obvious," Sir Paul replied.

He sprang forward without warning and slashed at Jack. Jack ducked and the sabre whistled over his head. He jumped out of range and defended himself as Sir Paul came at him again, cutting and thrusting skilfully. He was a powerful man, and the sheer weight of his attack forced Jack to give ground. The fight took them close to the practice dummy; Sir Paul aimed at Jack's head and swung it round. Somehow Jack parried the whirling blades, but Sir Paul's blow forced him to his knees. The nobleman hacked at him wildly, but Jack locked swords and, with a sudden, mighty heave, threw him to the ground.

Sir Paul glared up at him. "Finish me then!" he gasped.

Jack shook his head. "That's the difference between us," he panted.

Sir Paul struggled to his feet, then looked round in astonishment to see Sarah and Honesty; beside them stood Captain Tennant.

"Sir Paul Fisher?" said Tennant impassively.

"Your servant, sir," answered Sir Paul with as much dignity as he could muster.

"My name is Captain Tennant, sir. And I warn you that Miss Morton and I have heard everything that has passed between you and Mr Vincent."

"So? A pair of eavesdroppers, eh?" mocked Sir Paul. "I am surprised at you, Sarah!"

Sarah looked at him with disgust.

"Pray continue, Captain Tennant," said Sir Paul.

"I am empowered by His Majesty's Customs Commissioners and the Secretary of State – "

"Ah! How is Sir Edward? A dear friend of mine – but perhaps you're not aware of that."

"Empowered, I say," went on Tennant doggedly, "to take you into custody for conspiracy to murder and other charges."

"I would have thought murder was quite sufficient," interrupted Sir Paul.

" – other charges of which I am sure you are aware – " finished Tennant.

"I am aware you have no evidence, Captain."

"I have heard enough to justify your arrest," retorted Tennant, "and Colonel Ward's."

Sir Paul bowed. "Very well, my dear sir," he said politely. "You must do your duty, of course. But I warn that when I am cleared of these charges, as I have no doubt I shall be, I will make it my business to see that you are removed from any position of authority you may hold." He bowed again. "After you, sir."

Tennant bowed. "No, sir, after you. I have been after you for some time!"

Sir Paul led Tennant into the house, while Jack shook his head cynically. "He'll wriggle out of it," he said.

Jack, Sarah and Honesty returned soberly to the lonely cottage on the cliffs, and while Honesty went down to the cove to work on the *Mary Jane,* Jack and Sarah sat talking quietly by the fire.

"If we hadn't . . ." Sarah began. "If we hadn't known each other, you would never have become mixed up in this business."

"I'd saved the life of an Excise Officer," Jack replied. "I was already mixed up in it."

There was a long silence. Sarah sighed.

"You're a strange man," she said finally. "You abandoned a fine career in the navy: you turned your back on your family and friends; you live alone; you break the law, and help people you hardly know. And after all this time I still cannot tell whether you care anything for me at all."

Jack looked at her. He could see that she was close to tears. He took her hand gently. "I care for you more than I can ever say," he said quietly. "But my life now is so very different from yours. What can I give you? I cannot

155

give you happiness – only danger. Any day I may be caught by the Excise men or drowned at sea. I am a smuggler. I live for danger. I need the excitement of pitting my wits against those who seek to enforce the cruel laws of England; and the thrill of running in cargoes under their very noses. I'm my own master, with my own ship to take me wherever I choose to go. And one day I shall go, Sarah. One day I shall leave Quayhaven for ever. There are oceans I've never seen, and the whole world lies open to me." He looked at her. She wouldn't meet his eyes.

"My country isn't England. The unfurling of her flag no longer means anything to me. But the curling of the great Atlantic waves, and the light slanting under the clouds across the horizon as far as the eye can see – *that* has some meaning for me. And I know, beyond any doubts, that my country – my true country – is the sea."

Sarah wept silently: the tears ran down her cheeks and she made no attempt to stop them. She had lost him. But how could it be otherwise? She would have gone with him to the ends of the earth, but she knew this was an impossible dream.

She stood up and turned to him. "I love you," she said, "I shall always love you."

Then, before he could stop her, she left the cottage and walked away down the cliff path. Out at sea there was an ominous sound of thunder. Jack came to the door and watched her go in silence. She didn't look back.

DICK TURPIN

Richard Carpenter

The dare-devil hold-ups ...
The stirring adventures ...
The outrageous escapades ...
of the most famous highwayman of them all.

Dick Turpin is a brilliant rider and master
swordsman whose belief in liberty and his own
rough justice make him an outlaw in the
perilous and corrupt world of 18th century
England.

Here is the first book of Dick Turpin stories
based on the exciting TV series. Read how Dick
Turpin meets Swiftnick and outwits the
treacherous Sir John Glutton and his wily
steward, Captain Spiker, in a series of thrilling
and hilarious adventures.

Armada

From Alfred Hitchcock,

Master of Mystery and Suspense—

A thrilling series of detection and adventure. Meet The Three Investigators – Jupiter Jones, Peter Crenshaw and Bob Andrews. Their motto, "We Investigate Anything", leads the boys into some extraordinary situations – even Jupiter's formidable brain-power is sometimes stumped by the bizarre crimes and weird villains they encounter. But with the occasional piece of advice from The Master himself, The Three Investigators solve a whole lot of sensational mysteries.

Armada